"Can you give us the names of the men who were part of this morning's *minyan*?" asked Stella.

Glick hesitated, shrugged, and said, "Ten of us. Me, Asher, Rabbi Mesmur, Simon Aaronson, Saul Mendel, Justin Tuchman, Herman Siegman, Sanford Tabachnik, Yale Black, and Arvin Bloom."

"All regulars?" asked Aiden.

"All except Mendel and Bloom," said Glick. "I don't know Bloom. He came with one of the members, spent some time talking to my brother. Mendel still works. Can't always make it. The others are retired. The *minyan*, the *shul*, are their life."

"Is there some reason your brother would have stayed after the *minyan*?" asked Stella.

"No," said Glick, sipping his cup of coffee. "He had to get to work."

"He did say something about having to do something at the synagogue after the *minyan*," Yosele remembered. "He said it would take only a few minutes."

"It took more than a few minutes," said Glick, looking down. "It took his entire life."

CSI:NY™

BLOOD ON THE SUN

a novel

Stuart M. Kaminsky

Based on the hit CBS series "CSI: NY"
Produced by CBS Productions, a Business Unit of
CBS Broadcasting Inc. and
Alliance Atlantis Productions Inc.
Executive Producers: Jerry Bruckheimer,
Anthony E. Zuiker, Ann Donahue, Carol Mendelsohn,
Andrew Lipsitz, Danny Cannon, Pam Veasey,
Jonathan Littman
Series created by: Anthony E. Zuiker,
Ann Donahue, Carol Mendelsohn

POCKET
BOOKS

LONDON • SYDNEY • NEW YORK • TORONTO

An *Original* Publication of POCKET BOOKS

**POCKET
BOOKS**

Published by POCKET BOOKS, a division of
Simon & Schuster, Ltd
Africa House, 64–78 Kingsway, London WC2B 6AH

ISBN-13: 9781416511069
ISBN-10: 1-4165-1106-7

This Pocket Books paperback edition April 2006

10   9   8   7   6   5   4   3   2   1

POCKET STAR BOOKS and colophon are registered
trademarks of Simon & Schuster, Ltd.

Cover art by Patrick Kang

Printed and bound in Great Britain

A CIP catalogue record for this book is available
from the British Library

To the Krechmans—Sheldon, Carole and my lovable and loving Aunt Goldie.

The communication of the dead is tongued with fire beyond the language of the living.

—*T. S. Eliot*

Prologue

The STALKER WATCHED from the window of Seth's Deli, a copy of the *Post* open in front of him, a mug of decaf coffee in his hand. He had already paid in cash and left a twenty-percent tip. Once, a long time ago, he had waited tables. It had been a far different setting, but the dishes and cups had been just as dirty, with people leaving used napkins in which they had blown their noses or spat upon or stuffed into quarter-filled coffee cups.

He sat so that he could watch the glass doors of the building across the street. It was the perfect place to wait for her to come out. The problem was that he couldn't come here too often. He didn't want to be remembered, even though, given the morning swirl of waitresses and customers and the clanking of plates and the calling in of orders, it was unlikely he would be noticed.

The cliché was that New Yorkers were too self-absorbed and in a hurry to pay much, if any, attention to other people.

But most of the people around him were only New Yorkers because for the moment, for a few weeks, months, or years, they resided here. They were white, brown, black, or yellow, and many had either the hint of an accent or the thick coating of one from another part of the country, or another part of the world.

He, on the other hand, had been born in the city and, with only one long absence, had remained in it. His family had come over from County Cork in Ireland before the Civil War. He had relatives who had died in that war, and some every war since, including his father.

He was at home in the city. Or he had been until the person he was stalking had taken the life of the last person on earth he loved.

The double glass doors of the building across the street opened and she walked out. Another woman, whom he had seen with her before, was at her side, as was a man in a shirt and tie. The women were carrying blue plastic kits that looked vaguely like fishing tackle boxes. The man was empty-handed, but the Stalker knew that tucked into a holster at the back of the man's belt was a pistol.

He got up from the table, folded the newspaper

under his right arm and moved toward the door. He would make his notes in the book in his pocket as soon as he had time. He had filled eight identical books with notes. Those books sat in a neat pile in his dresser drawer, lined up chronologically. The first one began three months ago.

As he stepped into the morning heat and looked up at the sun, he felt a hint of satisfaction. The day would be hot, gritty. He would need a long shower and shampoo, but that would come later, much later.

Heat waves, like the one the city was presently going through, probably claimed more lives each year than floods, tornadoes and hurricanes combined. And the greatest human toll was in the cities, where the area of heat-absorbing dark roofs and pavements exceeds the area covered by cooling vegetation. Rural areas got some relief when temperatures dropped at night. The people of a city like New York were under further risk of health damage because of pre-existing stress on the body's respiratory and circulatory systems partly due to air pollution.

People were irritable, just as they had been in 1972 when New York suffered a two-week heat wave that claimed 891 lives. The Stalker had been here in 1972, but he did not remember suffering. Suffering had come twenty years earlier in a land far away, a land about which he cared little. The heat of 1972 had been no more than a minor annoyance. He remembered that the burning heat had kept people inside, cut his income in half for two weeks. Today people were also staying home. The present temperature was a humid 103 degrees. Power was failing as people turned on their air conditioners full blast. Emergency rolling blackouts were in effect.

He knew where the three people across the street were headed: the garage where the Crime Scene Unit cars were parked. His rental car, a dark blue Honda Civic, was parked directly in front of the deli in front of a fire hydrant. He would not be towed. He would get no ticket. He had turned down his sunshade so that the card he had placed there could be seen. The card read: EMERGENCY MEDICAL Treatment, CITY OF NEW YORK.

He used his remote button to open the car's doors and climbed into a chamber of searing heat. He removed the card from the sunshade, put it on the seat next to him and left the shade down.

He sat silently, savoring the moment of sudden, intense sauna heat before starting the car and turning on the air conditioner, which blew hot air into his face for a few seconds before starting to cool.

He did not delude himself as he drove slowly into traffic. He knew what he was. He was a stalker. Actually, he took pride in the title. He was good at it, had studied it. But he wouldn't be a stalker much longer. He would become an executioner, and the person whose photograph he now removed from his pocket and placed on the seat next to him would be the executed.

In the photograph—as in life—she looked serious, pretty, confident; a woman, not a girl. Stella Bonasera was her name, and she had made an error, a terrible, irreversible error, for which she would pay. Soon.

1

MAYBELLE ROSE WAS SCREAMING.

It was a little after eight on a Tuesday morning on an usually quiet street in Forest Hills, a few miles from Flushing Meadows Park and Shea Stadium. Maybelle, black, overweight, around fifty, was standing in front of a white two-story house.

In the house next door, Aaron Gohegan was shaving, his electric shaver almost silent. He heard the screams and, shaver in hand, moved to the bedroom window, past his wife, Jean, who, night mask over her eyes and purple plugs in her ears, snored gently.

Maybelle Rose was looking around frantically, her screaming mixed with weeping.

Aaron, currently in his undershirt and trousers and barefoot, always left for work in Manhattan at 8:15 a.m. It had been his routine for twelve years.

He had a reputation for punctuality and reliability, at fifty-two the youngest vice president at Raven-son Investments.

Today, he knew, as his eyes met Maybelle's, that reputation would suffer. Aaron put on the neatly pressed white shirt he had hanging on the closet door, slipped on his socks and shoes and headed out of the bedroom and down the stairs.

Behind him, his wife was dreamily saying something he didn't understand.

Maybelle was screaming louder now, hoarse, frantic, looking around for help as Aaron stepped through his front door.

As Aaron ran across the lawn toward Maybelle, Maya Anderson, the seventy-one-year-old widow who lived across the street, also hurried toward the screaming woman.

As the two neighbors came closer they could see thick beads of sweat on Maybelle's face.

Maybelle, who weighed almost 250 pounds, sagged into the arms of Maya Anderson, who weighed slightly more than 150. Amazingly, the older woman managed to hold up the now sobbing woman until Aaron stepped in to help.

On wobbly thick legs, Maybelle, gasping for air, turned her eyes toward Aaron, a pleading look on her face.

"What happened?" asked Maya gently.

Maybelle turned her head toward the older

woman and tried to speak. Nothing came out but a dry rasp and something that might have been a word.

Aaron and Maya gently sat Maybelle down on the lawn. She was breathing rapidly, trying to catch her breath. Then she said, "Dead."

"Dead?" Aaron repeated. "Who?"

"All of them," Maybelle said, looking over her shoulder at the house behind her.

The door to the house was open. Aaron, who had been a medic in the first Gulf War, rose and turned toward the house. Maybelle's breathing was even harsher now. She reached for her chest and muttered, "Oh my sweet Jesus."

"I think she's having a heart attack," Aaron said, reaching into his pocket for his cell phone.

"The devil came to that house," Maybelle whispered.

"Don't talk," said Maya as Aaron punched in 911.

But Maybelle had one more thing to say.

"The blood, sweet Jesus. They are washed in the blood of the lamb. They're floating in the blood of the lamb. The devil . . ."

Aaron decided not to enter the house until the police arrived.

Six hours earlier, Danny Messer had gotten on an A train. There was no one in the car but Danny, who put down his backpack, sprawled on a seat, took off his glasses and rubbed the bridge of his nose.

He had spent the last sixteen hours, with two short breaks, looking at maggots, most of which had been found in the torn stomach cavity of ten-year-old Teresa Backles. Teresa's body had been buried under garbage in a Dumpster behind a subsidized apartment complex in Harlem. There were times when the garbage wasn't picked up for a week or more. This had been one of those times. The heat had accelerated the growth of the maggots and the decomposition of the girl's body.

Danny put his glasses back on and closed his eyes, seeing crawling white maggots. They were the Crime Scene Investigator's friend, revealing secrets of the dead, but that didn't stop Danny from thinking that someday he . . .

He had determined that the girl had died five days earlier. He could almost pinpoint the hour. The maggots were sometimes better at that than the medical examiner, especially if you knew what you were looking for. Danny knew.

Danny had put on a mask and climbed into the Dumpster, going through every item, including rotting, ant-covered takeout food and a single skinny dead rat with its mouth open, showing its teeth.

Teresa's mother's boyfriend had lied about when he had last seen Teresa. The maggots had told

Danny. There was no mistake. The boyfriend, twenty-two-year-old Cole Thane, when confronted with the evidence, which included a single finger-print on the outside of the Dumpster, had talked. He had planned to rape the girl and then kill her, but when the time came, he couldn't do it—a rapist-murderer of children with a conscience. So he had only killed and mutilated the child instead.

Cole Thane had searched Dannys eyes for sympathy.

A pill and a few hours' sleep and Danny would be ready to go back to work. The crime scenes didn't stop. They piled up. Bodies: fresh, decayed, surprised, at peace. More every day.

Was the search for the killers motivated by justice, revenge, morbid curiosity or professional pride?

Maggots. Cole Thane looking for sympathy. Danny's arm, the arm he had thrown out in his try-out for the majors, began to ache. Nothing new.

The air-conditioning in the subway car was running at about half power. Danny's wrinkled white shirt clung to him. He could feel the drops of sweat dripping down his chest and stomach.

A shower. A pill. Some sleep.

To Danny's right, the door between cars opened. He slowly sat up, languidly put his right hand on top of his backpack.

The two who had come in were Hispanic, no more than twenty, one lean, one muscled up. They wore identical black T-shirts with a single letter "T" in white over the heart.

There was a chance they would walk past Danny, but Danny Messer was from the streets above and, in the tunnels below, he knew better. They were only a few feet from him now.

Danny felt something—not fear, but something he hadn't felt in years. The feeling mixed with the flashing images of crawling maggots, a little black girl in a Dumpster covered in dried blood and maggots, Cole Thane convincing himself he deserved mercy.

The two young men stopped in front of Danny. The lean one took a knife out of a sheath in his pocket. The stocky one had a short lead pipe in his hand.

Danny's backpack was jammed with heavy books. He swung it at the stocky man as he rose. He swung it hard, with an animal grunt.

At six in the morning, Mac Taylor sat alone at a table in Stephan's Deli on Columbus, a copy of *The New York Times* in front of him. He had taken his usual three-mile morning run in Central Park at dawn before the sun gathered strength.

It was scheduled to get up to a humid 100 degrees by noon. Mac had finished his eggs over easy, wheat toast and small orange juice and was working on his second cup of coffee while he read.

Stephan's wasn't crowded; there were about a

dozen people at the counter and the six tables. He wouldn't be bothered at Stephan's. The waitresses respected his faraway look. They knew he was a cop who saw things they prayed they would never have to see.

Connie, approaching sixty, with an ever-present weary smile, came to fill Mac's cup. He nodded his thanks.

"Gonna be a hot one," Connie said.

Mac nodded as he lifted his cup to drink.

"Got a busy day today?" she asked.

Mac met her lonely eyes and smiled.

"Not yet," he said.

His cell phone rang. Mac took it out of his pocket and said, "Taylor."

He listened and Connie stood nearby, hoping to keep contact with the soulful policeman, who said, "On the way."

He flipped the phone closed, took a ten-dollar bill and two singles from his wallet, placed them next to the check Connie had left, and got up from his seat.

"Bad?" she asked.

"Bad," Mac confirmed.

Danny Messer pushed his glasses back up his nose and listened to NPR as he drove. Traffic was heavy. It was always heavy in Manhattan, but he knew ways to get around it. It was his city.

Danny had managed four hours of troubled sleep. He hadn't dreamed about the dead little girl or what he had done to the two men on the subway.

Instead he dreamed about an incident that had occurred more than a month earlier when he had worked a rape-murder case. The victim, fifteen, had been torn up badly during the rape, her eyes gouged out. Then the killer had left the body in an alley, where the rats had gotten to it.

The killer had left his semen, and identifying him had been routine. The murderer's name was Lenny Zooker and he had already done five years for rape. He had been in his one-bedroom ratty apartment on 98th Street watching a rerun of *The Andy Griffith Show* when Danny and Don Flack came to pick him up. He was gaunt, cadaverous, his hair thin and brushed back. Teeth uneven. Eyes a moist brown.

Zooker had smiled as he let them in. In the middle of the room was the body of a ten-year-old girl and a thick pool of nearly black, fly-covered blood.

Zooker looked at the blood. Splatters of it covered the floor and shabby furniture.

"Haven't had time to clean up," Zooker said apologetically. "Should have. Was expecting you."

Danny had let out a grunt of pain and punched the grinning killer in the face. Zooker fell back, tripping, slipping in the dead girl's blood.

Now, in the car heading for Queens, he looked at his right hand. There was a definite tremor. It had begun when he woke up this morning. It had begun after dreaming about Lenny Zooker and those two dead girls.

In his dream, he willed them to live, to get up from the blood that shrouded them. Debbie, fifteen; Alice, ten. Danny had willed them to live, and just when he was sure Debbie's right hand had twitched, Danny woke up drenched in sweat, jaws aching, hand twitching. It had been 6:40 a.m. Danny had gotten up. He didn't want to sleep. He didn't want to dream.

Forty minutes later, Danny pulled into a parking spot behind Mac's car. This was a neighborhood in Forest Hills of well-kept, large old houses with matching immaculate lawns, far in distance and space and safety from where Danny had grown up. He got out of the car, first reaching back to get his evidence kit, and moved through the crowd of curious bystanders toward Mac, who was also carrying a kit, standing at the front door.

"What happened?" asked one woman with dyed red hair, wearing a robe she held close to her with both hands.

Danny didn't answer.

A uniformed officer stood at the front door. Both Mac and Danny had taken out their CSI ID badges and hung them around their necks. Danny had made a fist to conceal the tremor, which seemed to be getting worse.

"What have we got?" Mac asked the officer, whose name tag read WYCHECKA.

Wychecka couldn't have been more than twenty-five.

"Multiple," said Wychecka. "Upstairs. Two detectives in there, Defenzo and Sylvester."

"No one else comes in here," said Mac. "No one. Not even you."

Wychecka nodded.

Mac nodded back and moved past the officer with Danny behind him. Both men reached into their pockets and pulled out latex gloves. Danny had trouble getting his on.

"You okay?" asked Mac.

"Fine; let's work."

Mac looked at Danny, who took a camera from his kit and started up the stairs, taking photographs as he moved.

They could smell death, could smell blood as they moved up to the second-floor landing of the house.

The house was sunlight bright, furnished with comfortable antiques, solid, slightly ornate, expensive. The air-conditioning was running on high.

They walked on the well-polished wooden floor toward the sound of voices coming from one of the bedrooms. The door was open. On the bed were two female bodies, bloody bodies, hands folded across their chests, heads resting on pillows, eyes closed. The older of the two wore colorful Chinese pajamas. The younger victim wore only an XXXL T-shirt with USHER printed on it over the picture of a young black man whose mouth was open, singing a silent song to the dead. On the floor, collapsed on his right side, legs at odd angles, eyes open, was a man in a blood-drenched white terry cloth robe.

The two detectives on the scene greeted the CSIs with a shake of the head.

"Defenzo," the older one, short, solid, gray hair brushed back, said.

The other detective was younger, black, no more than thirty, with TV-star good looks. He was introduced as Trent Sylvester.

Mac handed each of the detectives a pair of latex gloves. They put them on, something they should have done when they entered the house.

Danny took photographs of the bodies and the room and placed his kit on the floor while Defenzo said, "Two on the bed are Eve Vorhees, mother of victim two, Becky Vorhees, seventeen. Man on the floor is husband and father, Howard Vorhees."

Mac carefully collected blood samples on cotton swabs and dropped them gently into sealable plastic bags, which he deposited in his kit while Danny took photographs.

Mac looked around the room. It was a teenage girl's room, filled with makeup and small framed photographs of young boys and girls mugging for the camera. Becky Vorhees, blond, pretty, was in all the photographs, often with her tongue sticking out. Mac leaned over the dead girl and touched his wrist to her arm.

She felt warm and stiff, suggesting that she had been dead between three and eight hours. If she had felt warm but not stiff, Mac would have estimated she had been dead less than three hours. Cold and stiff meant she had been dead eight to thirty-six hours, and if she were cold and not stiff she would have been dead thirty-six hours or more. It was a forensic rule of thumb; not precise, but helpful.

A better sense of the time of death would come after Medical Examiner Sheldon Hawkes examined the bodies. As soon as the three members of the Vorhees family had died, organisms in their intestines became active and began attacking the intestines and the blood. Gas formation could lead to a rupture of the intestines, releasing the organisms to attack the other organs. Muscle cells deprived of oxygen produce high levels of lactic acid. This leads to a complex reaction in which the proteins that form our muscles, actin and myosin, fuse to form a gel, which stiffens the body until decomposition begins. The stiffening of the body, rigor mortis, is due to this chemical reaction.

By examining the body, Hawkes would be able to determine a more precise time of death, among other things, dependent on the degree of decomposition.

But there were many other things an autopsy could tell them, all of which meant that Mac and Danny had to be quick, be thorough and get the three bodies to the lab as quickly as possible.

Mac looked down at the body of Howard Vorhees, who hugged himself, either to hold in his rapidly flowing blood or to protect himself from another attack.

"Cleaning lady, Maybelle Rose, found them when she came in a few hours ago," said Sylvester. "She's next door at a neighbor's. We tried to question her, but she just kept crying."

"We'll talk to her," said Mac.

"Weapon?" asked Danny.

"We're looking for it," Defenzo said. "But that's not all we're looking for. There's one more member of the family, a twelve-year-old son, Jacob. We can't find him."

Stella Bonasera and Aiden Burn stood in a small synagogue library on Flatbush Avenue in Crown Heights, Brooklyn, and looked down at the body of a man who lay in the bright beam of morning sun that filtered through the only window in the room.

The black-bearded dead man wore a dark suit

and blue tie. He lay on his back, eyes closed, head turned to the right. The man was laid out on a chalked cross, his hands—palms up—and bare feet pinned to the wooden floor by thick nails. Crucified. Printed in chalk on the floor were words in Hebrew: *"Ein tov she-ein bo ra."*

Against one wall was a loose pile of thick, long, almost black nails. There was also a hammer next to the nails.

On this wall, in what looked to Stella like the writing of a different hand than the one that had written the Hebrew words, scrawled in white paint were the words CHRIST IS KING OF THE JEWS. Were there two of them, two killers?

In the immaculately clean sanctuary just outside the door to the library, Detective Don Flack spoke to the bearded man in black. Flack had written the man's name in his notebook, Rabbi Benzion Mesmur. Rabbi Mesmur wore a wide-brimmed black hat. His wrinkled, arthritic hands were folded in front of him.

"Who is he?" asked Flack, who longed for a cup of coffee.

He had slept later than usual and hadn't had time to heat a cup of yesterday's coffee in the coffeemaker, nor had he had time to pick up a carry-out cup of coffee from the Korean deli on the corner near his apartment. Flack was not happy about this turn of events.

"Asher Glick," said the rabbi, looking at the closed door behind which Stella and Aiden were going over the crime scene.

Flack wrote down the name. "You have an address for him?"

The rabbi nodded and said, "I'll get it, but it's not necessary. His wife is outside with the others. Her name is Yosele. His children are Zachary and Menachem."

The rabbi closed his eyes.

"What was he doing here?" asked Flack.

The rabbi shrugged.

"I don't know. Morning *minyan* was over. The men all left for work, home."

Flack wrote that down.

"You know what a *minyan* is?" asked the rabbi.

"At least ten men who've been bar mitzvahed gather every morning for prayers," said Flack.

"You're not Jewish," said the rabbi.

"No, but my best friend, Noland Weiss, was."

"We had a Noland Weiss in our congregation years ago," said the rabbi. "He left us to join the conservatives."

"And the police. We were partners."

The rabbi waited for more.

"He's dead," said Flack. "Shooting during a routine drug bust. He saved my life." *F 2037930*

The rabbi closed his eyes, leaned forward and said something in Hebrew.

"You know anyone who might do a thing like this?" asked Flack.

"Perhaps."

"Who?"

" 'Thou shalt not bear false witness,' " said the rabbi. "If he is innocent, as he well may be, I will have borne false witness."

"Rabbi . . ."

"Ask Yosele, his widow," the rabbi said. "She is outside with the others. She is the pregnant woman with two small children certainly clinging to her. I should let them in."

"It's a crime scene. Do you know why there's a pile of nails and a hammer next to the wall near the deceased?" asked Flack.

"Repairs," said the rabbi.

"Asher Glick?"

The rabbi nodded with understanding.

"Asher Glick was a respected member of our congregation," said the rabbi. "Devout without being pedantic."

"What did he do for a living?" Flack said, looking at the *bimah*, the raised platform on which the simple pulpit sat. In the wall behind the *bimah* was a recessed alcove with a sliding wooden door.

"The Torah," said the rabbi, following Flack's eyes.

"The first five books of the Scriptures," said Flack. "Transcribed by a *sopher*, a scribe, by hand on a single sheet of parchment using a quill pen. He devotes his life to slowly hand-printing the five books on a scroll. And if he makes even the smallest error, he has to discard the scroll and start again."

"It must be pristine," said the rabbi. "Like life, there is no going back. We have four Torahs. Your partner taught you something of our religion."

"A little," said Flack. "What did Mr. Glick do for a living?"

"Furniture," said the rabbi. "He bought antique furniture at estate sales, shops, usually from people who had no idea of the value of what they were selling. I am told he had a brilliant eye for what lay beneath a veneer of paint, polish, misadventures and neglect. He then found buyers who he knew would be interested in his acquisitions and the buyers would restore the pieces and sell them."

Inside the library, Stella and Aiden looked down at the body. It was time to call the paramedics and have them take the dead man away.

But Stella found herself studying the corpse. Something was wrong. They had missed something.

"How long has he been dead?" Stella asked.

Aiden had taken the dead man's temperature.

"About two hours," Aiden said.

"Those nails wouldn't have killed him," Stella said. "And he didn't call for help."

Stella knelt next to the body and gently lifted the head. Beneath it was a small pool of blood. Aiden had examined the body. Aiden had missed it.

Aiden knew why she had missed it. No sleep. Up all night in bed. Not alone. This morning, still hazy after two cups of coffee, she had been thinking of ways to tell him that it was over, that she didn't want to see him again. She wanted to let him down without pain, but she hadn't thought of a way. What she had done was foul up on the job.

"Bullet holes in the back of the head," said Stella. "Close together. No exit wounds."

She looked at Aiden, who was staring at the corpse.

"No harm, no foul," said Stella. "You all right?"

Aiden nodded, went for her kit to take more photographs and to vacuum the dead man's clothes. She also took samples of the thin layer of sawdust on the floor next to a makeshift carpenter's bench.

Three minutes later Aiden and Stella came out of the library. In addition to their kits, Aiden carried a plastic bag with a hammer inside and another one filled with nails. Stella carried the now folded chair.

The old rabbi and Flack were waiting for them, steaming cups of coffee in their hands. Aiden moved toward the door at the back of the synagogue to call in the paramedics.

"What do those Hebrew words mean?" asked Stella. "The ones printed by the body."

"*Ein tov she-ein bo ra,*" said the rabbi. " 'There is no good with no evil in it.' It's a Kabbalah saying."

"So the killer was Jewish," said Flack.

"Not necessarily," said the rabbi. "The sole purpose of those words in Hebrew may well have been to make you think the killer was a Jew."

"You'd make a good detective," said Flack.

"The Talmud teaches us to be wary of simple answers," said the rabbi. "When can we have the body?"

"Maybe three days," said Stella.

"Unacceptable," said the rabbi. "He must be buried by tomorrow."

"Wrapped in a linen shroud," said Flack. "In a plain pine box. No embalming."

"He must be returned to the earth from which he came as soon as possible," said the rabbi.

"We'll try to get the autopsy done today," said Stella.

The rabbi was shaking his head "no."

"He must not be cut open, his organs removed," the rabbi said. "He must go naked and whole as he came."

"I'm afraid an autopsy is necessary," Stella said gently as two paramedics entered the synagogue, wheeling an aluminum cart that rattled and echoed loudly through the room.

"We will fight this," said the rabbi as he looked soulfully at the two paramedics.

"Many Orthodox Jews have had autopsies," said

Flack. "Our medical examiner will be as unobtrusive as possible."

"But still he invades," said the rabbi. "We have lawyers. We will try to stop you."

"You'll fail," said Stella.

"I know," said the rabbi, "but since when is the certainty of failure a reason not to try?"

"We'll need the names of the other men at this morning's *minyan*," said Flack.

The rabbi shook his head.

"I cannot without their permission," he said.

"Then I'll get them another way," said Flack.

It was time to remove the nails in the hands and feet of Asher Glick. Stella returned to the small library, and with the help of the paramedics, she did just that, talking into a miniature tape recorder, indicating the depth of each wound through the body and into the floor. Then the paramedics exited the library, pushing the cart on which the body of Asher Glick now lay covered by a white sheet.

The rabbi watched as the cart was wheeled down the center aisle.

"If I get the names of those in the *minyan* another way, it'll take time, time I could be spending looking for Mr. Glick's killer," said Flack.

"I cannot," said the rabbi.

Flack gave up, put his hands on his hips and looked at Stella, who shrugged. They'd get nothing more here, not now.

"They should have sent a Jewish detective," the rabbi said softly, more to himself than Flack, Stella and Aiden.

No one said anything, but all three agreed.

"I should—must—go out to the congregation, bring them in," said the rabbi, leaning forward.

"It's a crime scene," said Flack. "You can't bring them in for a few hours."

The rabbi nodded and said, "Talk to Yosele. She is outside."

There was nothing more to say. The three investigators headed for the door, opened it and found themselves facing a crowd of bearded men of all ages, all wearing black suits and wide-brimmed black hats. The women had their heads covered by scarfs, and many of them herded children together. Behind this first crowd was another, smaller crowd of curious, young, mostly male black people.

Crown Heights had been the site of more than four days of rioting in August of 1991 after an ultra-Orthodox Lubavitcher Jew drove his car into two black children. The African-American blacks and the growing number of Caribbean blacks joined in the riots and the attacks, focusing their rage not on whites, not on all Jews, but solely on the ultra-visible sect in black hats, suits and beards. Many in the black community had believed for years that these Jews got special treatment from the city. The belief erupted on that hot August night. Flack, a rookie cop, had been sent with hundreds of others to the 71st Precinct with full riot gear.

Tensions had grown somewhat less strained over the years, but they had not disappeared.

Had they heard that Asher Glick had been crucified? Flack was considering calling in the potential situation when a woman shouted, "Joshua" from the middle of the crowd of one hundred or more people.

The crowd picked up the chant, and the name "Joshua" echoed through the narrow street.

One of the men in the crowd, who was not dressed in black, and who did not pick up the chant, stood with one hand at his side and one in his pocket and watched the door. The hand in his pocket touched a photograph of Stella Bonasera.

2

"No sign of the boy," Danny said. "No sign of the knife. We did find this."

He held up a thick see-through sealed plastic bag. Inside the bag were dozens of pieces of colored glass. Mac took the bag and held it up to the light.

"I used the spectroscope," Danny went on. "No sign of any blood on the fragments. Not surprising, since they were all killed with a knife, but . . ."

"I'll take this back to the lab," said Mac.

Danny and Mac were standing outside the bedroom where the dead were lying. Mac looked over the wooden railing and down at the polished wooden floor of the living room. The sofa was a dark green. Two oak, brown leather armchairs with matching hassocks. A solid, dark oak coffee table and standing lamps with glass shades. A large, colorful rug that looked handmade and Native American lay at an angle on the floor. A single, large gold-framed painting on the wall, the Vorhees family, about five or six years old. The girl was no more than twelve, the boy about seven. All were looking directly forward, displaying the same artificial smile that failed to capture anything about what any of them were thinking or feeling.

Danny followed Mac's gaze and looked at the painting. Mac didn't look at him as he said, "When we get back you make an emergency appointment to see a department psychologist about that tremor."

Mac also noticed—but said nothing about—the raw, red bruises on Danny's knuckles.

Danny searched for something to say, but couldn't come up with anything. Besides, Mac was right.

In the parents' bedroom, Mac found a framed nine-by-eleven color photograph of the entire family. The parents were seated and smiling. The children stood behind them, also smiling. All the smiles were those of people who had been told to smile, the same smile Mac and Danny had seen in the painting in the living room.

"Recent," Danny said, looking at the photograph. "The girl looks about the same."

Mac agreed and kept looking at the photograph. "Possible scenarios?"

Danny adjusted his glasses, looked at the photograph.

"The boy killed them and ran," he said.

"But?" asked Mac.

"But, the kid's no more than one hundred pounds, puny," said Danny. "Whoever did this picked up the two women and placed them on the bed. The mother weighs at least 150. The daughter weighs about 120. Blood drops but no drag marks. Whoever did this picked up the women, placed them gently on the bed and folded their arms, which leaves out the boy."

Mac nodded. Danny didn't know what the nod meant.

"Intruder," tried Danny. "Came in to rape the girl, got caught by the mother and father, killed everyone, felt guilty and laid out the women."

"You checked the windows?" asked Mac.

"No sign of forced entry. Windows all locked."

"How did he get in?" asked Mac.

"Don't know yet," answered Danny.

"And the boy?"

"Saw or heard what happened," said Danny. "Ran. Or the killer caught him and decided not to kill him, at least not here."

"Why?" asked Mac.

"Hostage," said Danny. "Or . . ."

"Pedophilia," said Mac. "Get all the samples to the lab. Tell Jane to get the DNA run as fast as possible."

"I'd better get to the lab," Danny said as they went downstairs.

"Psychologist," Mac reminded him.

Danny didn't speak.

"As soon as you get back," said Mac.

The front door opened and Detective Defenzo stepped in.

"Side door of the garage is wide open," he said from the living room. "Cleaning lady says the boy has a bike. There's no bike in the garage."

"I'll check it before I leave," said Danny, starting down the stairs.

Mac nodded an okay and moved down the hall. They had already gone over the other bedrooms. No blood, everything in place in the parents' room. Clothes neatly hung in the closet, bathroom clean with white towels hung symmetrically on white plastic rods.

The boy's room was small, relatively neat, with a pair of jeans and a shirt slung over a chair that faced a computer on a cluttered desk. The white light on the computer was on, indicating the unit was asleep. The bed was unmade, blankets thrown back, pillow crumpled.

The walls were surprisingly bare except for a large poster of a group of four young men who looked out at the world as if they had a dirty secret. A single word, "Coldplay," was written in script at the top of the poster. A large cluttered metal book-case stood next to the bed. Mac picked up a book, one of the Harry Potters. A second book was a biography of John Glenn. The third book he picked up was different. The dust jacket of the book said it was *The Tick-Tock Man of Oz.* Mac opened it. It was definitely not about the Oz the dust jacket promised. It was a book about clinical sexual behavior.

Mac rechecked the boy's room for blood traces and found none. On the way to the boy's closet, he almost missed a small leaf no larger than a baby's fingernail in the threads of a bath mat–sized blue throw rug in the middle of the room. Mac bent, picked up the leaf with tweezers from his kit and deposited it in a plastic bag.

The closet was a mess of clothes piled on the floor and more clothes on hangers, the pants wrinkled, the shirts unbuttoned.

Mac was done here, for now. It was time to talk to the living, listen to the dead and ask questions of the evidence.

In the Gohegan home next to the house of the dead, the young black detective Trent Sylvester was alone in the living room with Maybelle Rose. He spoke to her gently and held her hand.

When Mac entered, the woman looked up fearfully.

"It's all right," said Sylvester. "He's one of us. A police officer."

An untouched glass of water already dancing with dust in the morning sunlight rested on the table next to the sofa on which Maybelle Rose sat.

"Never saw anything like that," she said.

"Almost no one has," said Mac, sitting on the arm of a chair next to the stunned woman. "How long have you worked for the Vorhees family?"

"Two years," she said. "Is he . . . ?"

"We haven't found him yet," said Mac.

"He's a good boy," she said. "They were all good to me, my family."

"Any of the family have enemies?" asked Mac.

"None," she said. "Good people. Not church people, but good people."

"Relatives?" Mac asked.

"None I heard of," said Maybelle.

"They ever fight?" he asked.

"Not much," she said, looking at Sylvester for reassurance.

"What did they fight about?" asked Mac.

"Becky's boyfriend," she said. "Name's Kyle Shelton. Mr. Vorhees thought he was too old for her."

"How old is he?"

"Don't know. Maybe twenty-five. He was always nice to me the few times I saw him."

"Know where he lives?" asked Mac.

"No," she said.

"He have a car?"

"He does," she said. "Some kind of blue pickup truck, you know? Dented fender on the passenger side. Don't know what make."

"Anything else you can tell me about the truck?"

"License number," she said. "Easy to remember. BEAST 1."

"Could you come back to the house with me and tell me if you notice anything missing, particularly a knife?" Mac asked.

"They still in there?" she asked, looking toward the hall, beyond which stood the house of the dead.

"Yes, but we won't go back till the paramedics take them away in a few minutes."

"I can wait," she said, reaching for the glass of water.

When Mac got up, the front door opened and Detective Defenzo stepped in.

"I think we have a witness," he said.

Lying in bed, she could hear the sounds of the city street traffic rumbling by even with the air conditioner on full blast. She was fully clothed, in a loose-fitting white cotton dress with odd, almost symmetrical patterns of color that reminded her of the works of Piet Mondrian.

She had been an art major, had painted, but knew she wasn't good enough or daring enough to make even a small scratch in the Manhattan art market.

The television set was on, but she had turned off the sound. She closed her eyes and put her left arm over her eyes to block out the sun and the world.

She was going to be forty-three on her next

birthday. She knew she looked at least ten years older. She was eleven pounds overweight and had no plans for losing any more.

The woman did not consider herself a failure. She certainly didn't consider herself a success either. She simply went through each day with books, trips to the Museum of Modern Art. Once she had enjoyed cooking. No more. Carry-out food was cheap, close by.

Her father, a big man, had been in army intelligence during and after the Korean War. He had always worn an accepting smile that suggested that he knew things others, especially his children, would never know and would be better off not knowing. When he had died in his room, he had insisted on being alone and having no clergy at his side. She didn't even know if he believed in God or had been born into any religion.

What did she know of him beyond that? His favorite food was duck. His favorite movie was *Wild Boys of the Road*. He read *The New York Times* from cover to cover every day that he was home. He seemed to be content with whatever television show the family wanted to watch. She had no idea if he had been a Republican, a Democrat or a Socialist.

Her mother, shaped not unlike the woman in the bed was now, had clearly loved her husband, had spent her days teaching at the local elementary school and writing in her diary. She had been born a Methodist. As far as the woman in the bed knew, her father had never tried to talk his wife out of her religious beliefs. She had simply let them slide away.

She heard footsteps coming up the stairs, light, almost noiseless. There was no point in pretending to be asleep. He would know.

Just as she had known, when her father had come back from one of his "duties" out of the country, that the man coming up the stairs had done something or seen something about which she would never learn.

The footsteps were at the top of the stairs now. The door opened.

"Tea," he said, holding out the tray with the small blue-and-white pot and the matching cup and saucer.

She looked up.

Yes, he wore the same look she had seen on the face of her father when he had returned from one of his "duties." The next few days would be dark.

She sat up, accepting the offered tray.

She strongly suspected that he had killed. She strongly suspected that he would soon be doing so again. Maybe it was her imagination, but they had been together for so much of their lives that she could sense it.

And he was well aware that she could sense it.

*　　*　　*

Defenzo and Mac walked across the street to the house of Maya Anderson. It was well maintained, recently painted, probably the most modest house in the neighborhood.

The gawkers, not many of them, were still there. Now they were watching the paramedics take out their cart and wheel it into the Vorhees house. It would be the first of three carts and the crowd would be thrilled, frightened, repulsed, and happy that they were still alive as each draped body was removed from the house. They would have a story to tell, something new to fear, something that could become part of the backlog of stories that almost everyone carried with them.

Maya Anderson opened the door immediately. Her gray hair was cut short and she wore jeans and a green long-sleeved shirt over her compact body. She was definitely more than seventy; her bright green eyes revealed a dancing intelligence.

She ushered them in, moved ahead of them to a small kitchen, motioned for them to sit and asked what they wanted to drink. "Coffee, Diet Coke, water, a beer, schnapps?"

"Nothing, thanks," said Mac.

Defenzo accepted a Diet Coke.

When they were all seated, Maya, hands folded in front of her, said, "I garden."

She looked over her shoulder out the window,

where Mac could see a colorful array of blue, red, white and yellow flowers.

"I garden, read, watch HBO, take long walks and snoop on my neighbors," she said. "Used to be a bank manager. I don't sleep very much, which gives me a lot of time at the front window reading, watching old movies and seeing what's going on."

"What went on last night?" asked Mac.

"Morning. Around two. Vorhees girl's boyfriend pulls up in his pickup truck, parks down the block in front of the Packers', driver gets out and walks back to the Vorhees house. Goes in back."

"The pickup truck?" asked Defenzo, working on his Diet Coke.

"Blue," the woman said. "Dent on the right side."

"The man?" asked Mac.

"Sort of tall. White. Dark hair. One of those swaggerers, you know? Can't be sure if it was the boyfriend, too dark, but it definitely looked like him and he was driving his truck."

"Boyfriend come here often?" asked Mac.

"I probably shouldn't say," Maya answered with a sigh, "but what the hell. He'd drop the girl off in the afternoon, after school."

"Last night?" asked Mac.

Maya Anderson nodded somberly.

"Maybe some noise a few minutes after the

boyfriend goes in through the back," she said. "Hard to tell. My eyesight's good, but my hearing leaves something to be desired. Besides, that old house has thick walls and windows. To tell the truth, I think I dozed off for a few minutes. Then I heard a car door open, got my glasses on and saw the boyfriend's pickup go riding off."

"Which way?" asked Mac.

"That way," she said, pointing, "toward Queens Boulevard." Queens Boulevard fed directly into the Queensboro Bridge to Manhattan.

"Why didn't you call the police?" asked Defenzo, finishing his drink. Maya rose, took the can and dropped it into a covered receptacle marked RECYCLE.

"Over the last four years I've called the police fourteen times," she said. "Family fights, televisions turned too loud, dogs walking without leashes and pooping without anyone picking it up, Parker Niles from the next block drunk and throwing rocks at the streetlights, things like that. They don't take me seriously anymore."

"Thank you, Mrs. Anderson," said Mac, standing.

"They're all dead, aren't they?" she asked.

"We haven't found the boy yet," said Mac.

"I hope the boy got away," she said.

"We're going to find out," said Mac.

Instead of heading for his car, Mac crossed the street with Defenzo at his side, paused in front of the Vorhees house and looked around at the trees. For the next fifteen minutes, Mac inspected every tree on the Vorhees property and every one two houses down on either side of it.

Finally, he stopped, looked up and down the street.

"What?" Defenzo finally said, unable to hold it in any longer.

"No match," said Mac, deep in thought.

"For what?" asked Defenzo.

Instead of answering, Mac headed for his car, behind which the paramedic truck was parked. He paused for an instant as the paramedics brought out the first body.

Kyle Shelton drove.

To the world afraid of tomorrow and grieving over yesterday, he was Kyle Shelton, who knew how to put on clean jeans and a pressed long-sleeved shirt to hide his tattoos.

He knew the value of good teeth, had his own straightened, cleaned and whitened regularly and a nine-to-five haircut.

Even though he held a college degree, he now held down a job on the shipping dock of a super-sized hardware store in Manhattan, caused no trouble, smiled when the others laughed. A year of combat infantry in Iraq had changed him. Death, violent death, was now a part of his everyday experience.

He had earned his degree in philosophy at City University of New York. Kyle had been lucky enough to find a young professor with a Ph.D. from Brown to mentor him. The degree was validation, a sheet of paper he could show but never would. If he had ambition before, he had lost it in Iraq. He already knew more of philosophy than others he had seen graduate before him.

The sun had been up for a few hours. Kyle looked back in the general direction of Queens, back on what was lost forever. He had gone back to his one-room apartment on 101st, packed one large bag, and stopped for gas when he hit New Jersey, using his Visa card as payment.

He drove slowly. Cars, trucks passed him. He saw it all. Was it just hours ago? A dream? No dream. Becky, her mother, her father, dead. The knife. The knife sat on the seat next to him wrapped in paper towels. He hadn't decided what to do with it.

Just before three in the morning on the night before, in drenching heat and darkness, he had driven a mile, no more, saw the dirt path he was looking for in the wooded area next to the road, and turned onto it. After going a few feet, sure he couldn't be spotted from the road, he had parked, turned off his lights, got out of the car and with the flashlight from his glove compartment in hand, entered the thicket. He found what he was looking for, a clearing. He decided it would do and went back to the truck to get what he had placed in the back and covered with his stained canvas tarp.

No more than five minutes later, Kyle Shelton had stood in the darkness, looking at the bicycle on its side, front wheel bent. He had been through the wooded area. Signs of the boy—bloody shirt and pants, socks and even Nike sneakers—were spread out.

Kyle imagined the boy racing through the trees and bushes naked, wearing only his glasses, looking over his shoulder. He thought of the Truffaut movie *The Wild Child*, the supposedly true story of a boy who had lived all his life naked among the animals in a forest. Henri Poincare's words came to Kyle: "It is better to foresee, even without certainty, than not to foresee at all."

It hadn't been much of a plan, thought out at a moment's notice, full of holes. It might work. Probably not.

Kyle Shelton knew about fingerprints, DNA, blood samples. He didn't know much, but he knew enough. He wasn't safe.

There had been a half moon and some light from passing cars beyond the bushes. He imagined the boy, shivering, not from the night cold but from fear and horror, imagined that he had taken off all his clothes but not his glasses. Shelton got back in his pickup, backed off the dirt path to the road and headed for the bridge, headed for his small room. The running had begun.

"Mrs. Glick?" Stella said, approaching the woman in the crowd.

Both children at her side were boys with *yarmulkes* and locks of hair hanging down in front of their ears.

Yosele Glick looked up at Stella. Her eyes were bright, wary, a deep brown. She was fair-skinned, pretty, no more than thirty years old. At her side stood a mountain of a man in black with a massive girth, rimless glasses perched on his nose. His beard was full, dark and curly.

The small crowd of men, women and children moved close to Stella and Aiden to hear what was being said.

"Can we go somewhere quiet where we can talk?" asked Stella.

Yosele looked at the massive man at her side who said, "Timken's."

"You are?" asked Aiden.

"Hyam Yussel Glick," the man said. "Asher was my brother. You are detectives?"

"Crime scene investigators," said Stella.

"They had no men to send?" said Glick.

"They're working other cases," said Stella. "Timken's?"

The man led the way across the street, and traffic

stopped. Glick held up a hand to signal to the crowd that he should not be followed. A lean old man hurried out of the crowd ahead of them.

Timken's was a modest storefront kosher restaurant with the name written in Hebrew and English.

The old man who had broken away from the crowd used one of the keys from the chain he removed from his pocket to open the front door, and stood back so they could enter.

There was a murmur of voices from the street and a single word: "Joshua." Then the door closed and there was silence. Glick moved to a round table. There was no question about using a booth. Glick was too large. They sat and the overhead lights tinkled on.

The younger of the two boys standing next to the seated Yosele was sobbing. She comforted him with a hand on his head.

"Zachary," said Glick, "can you take your brother to the back room? Mr. Schwartz will bring you some cookies."

Behind the counter where he where brewing some tea, old Schwartz nodded. The two boys reluctantly left their mother's side. When they were gone, Stella asked, "Who is Joshua?"

"A zealot with a false and mad cause," said Glick.

"Joshua is a messianic Jew," Yosele said softly as the old man set out tea and rugalach. "A test brought on us by the Lord."

"He is not a Jew," Glick corrected.

"He claims to be a Jew who believes Jesus was the Messiah," said Yosele. "He and his followers, the Jewish Light of Christ, believe it is their mission to convince the most orthodox of Jews to accept Jesus."

"He is so mad that other messianics and Jews for Christ have renounced him," said Glick. "He opened a storefront temple two blocks down on Flatbush less than a year ago. He has no more than two dozen followers, but they come here, right here to the front of our synagogue, to hand out offensive flyers and try to engage our congregants in discussion. Since they come only a few at a time, the police can do nothing."

"And," said Stella, "your brother had conflicts with them?"

"Asher confronted them, argued with them, outshouted them," said Glick. "Persuaded, reasoned. He even got a few of them to renounce the idiocy of Joshua and move away."

"So Joshua was particularly upset with your brother?"

Glick stopped chewing a dark poppy-seed rugalach and said, "Less than a week ago, right across that street, Asher tried for perhaps the one hundredth time to reason with the lunatic. It ended with Joshua saying that my brother would be crucified like the ancient Hebrews for his unwillingness to accept the truth of the second coming."

"Can you give us the names of the men who were part of this morning's *minyan*?" asked Stella.

Glick hesitated, shrugged and said, "Ten of us. Me, Asher, Rabbi Mesmur, Simon Aaronson, Saul Mendel, Justin Tuchman, Herman Siegman, Sanford Tabachnik, Yale Black, and Arvin Bloom."

"All regulars?" asked Aiden.

"All except Mendel and Bloom," said Glick. "I don't know Bloom. He came with one of the members, spent some time talking to my brother. Mendel still works. Can't always make it. The others are retired. The *minyan* and the *shul* are their life."

"Is there some reason your brother would have stayed after the *minyan*?" asked Stella.

"No," said Glick, sipping his cup of coffee. "He had to get to work."

"He did say something about having to do something at the synagogue after the *minyan*," Yosele remembered. "He said it would take only a few minutes."

"It took more than a few minutes," said Glick, looking down. "It took his entire life."

"Did your husband say anything about what it was he had to do?" asked Stella.

"No," the widow said, "but I could tell that he wasn't looking forward to it."

Hyam Glick began to rock in his chair, eyes closed. He spoke softly in Hebrew.

Yosele translated, " 'Set me as a seal upon your heart, as a seal upon your arm. For love is as strong as death, passion fierce as the grave . . . Many waters cannot quench love, neither can the floods drown it.' "

"Song of Songs," said Stella.

Yosele nodded and looked at her now weeping brother-in-law.

Detective Trent Sylvester drove slowly down the road, letting traffic pass him. He concentrated on the right side, pausing whenever he saw anything that might be suspicious, finding nothing for thirty-five minutes. Then he came to the slight break in the bushes. He slowed down, parked and passed carefully through the opening.

In the clearing beyond the bushes, Sylvester saw the bicycle, front wheel twisted, handlebars turned almost around. He walked carefully for a few steps and then stopped, not wanting to contaminate the scene.

Beyond the bicycle lay a crumpled bloody white shirt next to a scattering of clothes—underwear, denim jeans, socks and a single sneaker. He scanned the ground looking for a second sneaker, but couldn't see it. Nor could he see the boy's body, but that could have been carried deeper into the trees or buried and covered with leaves.

Sylvester backed away, took his phone from his hip and called in what he had found. He was told, though he didn't have to be, to cordon off the crime scene.

Mac, who was still at the Vorhees residence when the call came in, arrived at the scene less than ten minutes later. Danny had already headed back to the lab with the samples they had taken.

"We start searching for the body?" asked Detective Defenzo at his side.

Defenzo felt the warm moist sweat under his arms and on his forehead. It wasn't even noon and his underpants were clinging and itching against his groin.

Mac didn't answer. He scanned the scene—bike, scattered clothes, shoe, ground. What he didn't yet see was the boy's second shoe and the glasses he always wore.

Mac opened his kit, pulled on his gloves and handed a second pair to Defenzo. Find the body, find the blood, find footprints, fingerprints, hair, anything.

But there was something else to look for. Mac was not ready to give it a name. The ground cover of leaves, hundreds, perhaps thousands, would make the search more difficult, but Mac was always suspicious when it was too easy.

He stepped forward and began his search, watching where he stepped, carefully reaching back to remove an insect from his neck, imagining

a frightened, pale, skinny twelve-year-old boy standing nude in this dark tiny clearing.

"Look for the boy," said Mac. "Watch where you
step. Touch nothing."

Defenzo nodded and headed into the trees to his
left.

Mac took photographs, knelt at each piece of evidence and examined it with a portable microscope
that looked nothing like the one Sherlock Holmes
used. The one in Mac's hand looked like a small
metallic pocket-sized eyeglass case. He went from
item to item, sometimes focusing the built-in tilting
light on something he enlarged by almost one hundred times.

For the next fifteen minutes, Mac gently picked
up leaves, examined them, and bagged them.

3

THE LARGE, DARKLY TINTED WINDOWS were emblazoned with the words THE JEWISH LIGHT OF CHRIST in neatly printed large gold letters. On the door were the words ENTER. ALL ARE WELCOME.

On the awning, down in front of both windows, were the faint remnants of the words GOLDMAN'S DRY CLEANING AND PROFESSIONAL TAILORING. The awning provided little relief from the angry sun.

Aiden and Stella had entered hoping to find air-conditioning. They found only a tired ceiling fan grinding away. Meanwhile, Flack had gone with Yosele Glick to her home to see if he could find names, leads, something to go on.

Inside the store fourteen chairs were in a half circle facing the door. All of the chairs were occupied. Seven men, seven women. The clean-shaven men in black all wore yarmulkes. The women all had their heads covered.

It struck both Aiden and Stella that these people were young, the oldest a man seated in the middle who might have been forty at the most.

The room was late-morning hot. The ancient ceiling fan turned slowly, making a tired scratchy sound.

"We've been expecting you," said the older man.

He was dark, lean, with thinning hair, a slightly pitted face and deep blue eyes that stayed focused on the two CSIs.

"Joshua?" asked Stella.

"I am," the man said. "And this is our congregation."

"All of it?" Stella asked.

"We will grow in numbers, faith and determination," he said. "There are fourteen million Jews in the world."

"Rabbi Mesmur says you've been harassing him and members of his congregation," said Stella.

The people seated in the other chairs barely moved. Some of them were now looking at Joshua with confident smiles.

"Our mission is to bring Jews to the true light of Christ as the Messiah," Joshua said. "To accomplish this, we must confront those who are misguided and convince them of the truth."

"Why?" asked Aiden.

"So they will be saved," said Joshua.

"A man was murdered in the temple this morning," said Stella.

"We know," said Joshua.

"Crucified," said Stella.

All eyes were now on the two women who stood before them.

"We'd like to collect your fingerprints and swab for DNA testing," said Aiden.

"We didn't kill anyone," said Joshua calmly. "We follow both the Commandments and the word of Christ the Savior."

"Then you won't mind our taking samples to eliminate you as suspects," said Stella.

"And did you do the same to the congregants at the *minyan* this morning?" asked Joshua. "Or Saint Martine's Church?"

"We're going to," said Aiden.

Joshua looked to those people seated at his right and said, "Devorah's father is a cantor in one of the largest orthodox congregations in Connecticut. David holds a doctorate in Jewish studies from Yale. Joel is an adjunct professor of classics at Columbia. Carole is a psychiatric social worker. Erik is a lawyer. Each of us knows the world beyond these walls. Each of us is committed to changing that world, saving those who will find peace only when they accept the word of Christ."

"Fingerprints," Aiden said calmly.

She had heard this kind of religious babble since she was a child and distrusted anyone with a hard religious line. She knew some of the religious zealots meant what they were saying, but often the words were a blanket over something dark beneath—seduction, money, power. Joshua struck Aiden as one who had secrets under his blanket of words. He also had the mad smile of certainty she had seen in true believers.

"We prefer not to," said Joshua, reaching out his hands on both sides and gently touching the shoulder of a girl on his right and a round-faced young man on his left.

"We can get a court order," said Stella.

"No," said a man on the left.

He was about thirty, wearing a suit and glasses.

"You don't have sufficient cause to compel us to comply," he said.

Joshua smiled, looked at Aiden and Stella and raised his eyebrows in victory.

"Erik . . . ," Joshua began.

". . . is a lawyer," Stella continued.

"No one in this congregation committed murder," Joshua said emphatically.

"I don't think we can simply take your word for that," said Stella.

"I did not imagine you would," said Joshua.

"And what were you before you found your religion?" asked Aiden.

"I was the son of a rabbi," said Joshua. "I was a writer of pornographic paperbacks, a lost soul. Now I have seen the light and the truth and am, myself, a rabbi, a teacher of the faith."

Devorah, the pretty, clear-skinned girl whose father was a cantor, rose and said, "You can take my fingerprints and a culture."

She did not look at Joshua, who nodded and said, "We are not a cult. If any member wishes to allow this, it is their choice."

David, lean, curly red hair, the one with the doctorate in Jewish studies, also rose and said, "I'll cooperate."

David looked at Joshua and said, "We have nothing to hide. We are in the hands of the Lord and will be saved."

Two others stood. Joshua was losing control and losing face in front of the two women. He looked at Stella. His mouth smiled but his eyes burned.

He rose, which prompted the rest of the small congregation to do the same.

There was a table against one wall. Aiden and Stella moved to it and asked the members of the congregation to line up. The process was reasonably fast, slowed down only by Stella searching the hands and clothing of each person for signs of blood or struggle and then checking the bottoms of their shoes for signs of blood or residue from the thin layer of sawdust at the murder scene. Aiden swabbed the inside of each person's cheek, bagged the swab and sealed and marked the see-through bag.

DNA, deoxyribonucleic acid, is composed of tightly bound strands called chromosomes. Humans have forty-six paired chromosomes, twenty-three from each parent. Two of these chromosomes decide gender. About thirty thousand genes are attached to each DNA strand. Among other things, genes make up the blueprint for who we are, how we function, our development and growth. No two samples of DNA are exactly alike.

Stella scanned each person with a portable Alternative Light Source. There were traces of blood on only one person in the group, a hefty dark-haired well-groomed young man who identified himself as Earl Katz.

"You have fresh blood on your hands," said Stella.

The young man, who towered over the two women, said, "Yes. A woman with a broken nose bled on me," he said. "Domestic disturbance. I'm a police officer. I got off duty about an hour ago, changed clothes, showered, took my uniform to the cleaner."

"We'll check," said Stella.

"I'm sure you will," said Earl Katz. "You wouldn't be doing your job if you didn't."

Joshua was last and best—traces of blood on

both hands and the bottoms of his shoes and what appeared to be patches of sawdust. Stella took samples of the blood and dust from the shoes.

"Want to explain this?" Stella asked, holding up the bags containing blood samples and samples of the sawdust.

"I prefer not to," said Joshua.

Stella took him in for questioning.

Medical Examiner Sheldon Hawkes was known to occasionally engage in gallows humor, but not today. He had the corpse of Becky Vorhees on the table before him. He had three more corpses in the sliding cabinets against the wall. It would be a long morning. Hawkes, an African-American, had recently been having dreams of walking through tall grass under a sun that looked too close. Ahead he could hear voices speaking in a language he didn't understand but was sure he once had. Hawkes wanted to run toward the voices but it was too hot. He was too tired. He finally made it through the grass and in the broad open space before him, three young bare-chested black men stood over a dead and bloody lion. The three men welcomed Hawkes, who moved toward them, knowing that his goal was the dead lion. It wasn't a bad dream at all.

Jane Parsons, who wore a white lab coat, blond hair dangling well-brushed down her neck, looked at the samples lined up on the large table in front of her. There were more than twenty samples. For years commercial laboratories had taken three to six weeks to run a DNA test. Gradually the testing time came down to three to seven days. Jane had cut the time to two days. If the samples were piling up and the CSI investigators were in a hurry, she could get it down to a day.

"Start with the daughter's blood," said Mac, leaning over her shoulder.

Was she wearing perfume? No. It was a combination of shampoo and conditioner. He backed away before . . . Jane looked over her shoulder at him.

"You all right?" she asked.

"Fine," said Mac. "How long will it take?"

"For all of this?" she said, looking at the table. "Two days. Can the budget take it?"

"It'll have to," he said, turning and walking across the room and through the glass doors.

Microscope in front of her, samples on her right, Jane began her work. She had the name of the willing or unwilling donor of each sample. She knew some of the donors had been murdered and others might be murderers. What she couldn't do, didn't want to do, was put bodies and faces and lives into the laboratory samples.

Using phenol and chloroform, she extracted the DNA from the first sample. She then precipitated the DNA with isopropanol. Next, under the electron microscope, she cut the DNA using restriction enzymes. This produced small DNA fragments. Jane then "loaded" the cut DNA onto an agarose gel that look like clear Jell-O. She mixed the gel and poured it into what looked like a rectangular baking dish. She moved on to the next sample. Each sample would have to sit for at least three hours before it could be used for the test.

When she had the completed gels for all the DNA samples, she would electrophorese the gel by running an electric current through it to separate the fragments according to their size. The fragments would be stained with ethidium bromide.

When this was done, she would be able to view separate fragments and compare the pattern to any DNA found at the crime scene. The separated fragments form the bar code pattern with which the public is familiar. She would end by taking photographs of the bar codes.

The work had to be done carefully. There were too many steps during which a mistake could be made. She assumed that Mac would want to submit the code to the FBI to search for and include in their CODIS (Combined DNA Index System).

Jane had a massive headache. When she could, she would take a few aspirin. The pain was familiar. It went with the job. Her eyes burned. Her mouth was dry. She kept on working.

*   *   *

Don Flack drank a cup of strong, heavily sweetened hot tea and listened to Hyam Glick, brother of the murdered man. They were sitting in the kitchen of Asher Glick's house, four blocks from the synagogue in which he was murdered.

More than a thousand observant Jews lived in the neighborhood, for many reasons. There was a sense of community, a wish to be near relatives, but most important, from sundown Friday to sundown Saturday, the Sabbath, they were forbidden to work or drive in cars. They were also required to attend services on both Friday night and Saturday morning. Far from ideal houses, many in the neighborhood were in need of major repair, but because of their location near the synagogue, when they went on the market, they sold for outrageous prices.

The Glick house seemed to Flack to need no work. The floors were even. The walls were clean, white and unscratched, the furniture unscuffed, the ceiling showing no signs of water damage or sagging.

Women were consoling Yosele and taking care of the children. Other men and women were preparing to sit *shivah*, covering mirrors, lining up chairs. Still others were out finding cakes, cookies and candy to set out on tables for those who would be coming to pay their respects and say the prayer for the dead.

"The *minyan*," Glick said with a sigh. "What can I tell you? I can imagine none of us doing a thing like this. Aaronson, Mendel, Tuchman and Siegman are over eighty. I can't see any of them overpowering my brother or having the strength to drive nails into his . . ."

Glick stopped, sighed and let out a sob. "My brother was a strong man," he said. "He worked with his hands, his back, moving, lifting furniture. He . . ."

Flack worked on his tea amid the bustle in the house and waited until Glick pulled himself together.

"Black has Parkinson's," Glick finally said. "Tabachnik and Bloom are young enough, no more than fifty, and reasonably healthy as far as I know."

"Are they regulars at the *minyan*?" asked Flack. He knew Glick had already shared this information with Aiden and Stella, but he wanted to hear it for himself.

"As I told your colleagues, all of those present were regulars, except for Mendel and Bloom."

"Your brother particularly close to any of these men?"

"To all of them. Asher was the solid rock of the congregation."

"What do these men do for a living?" asked Flack.

"All retired but me, Asher, Mendel and Bloom.

Mendel works in Schlosman's Kosher Bakery. He's a baker. His challah is acknowledged as the best in the city."

"Bloom?"

"I know little of him. He's new. I think he's in the furniture business like Asher. Seems like a nice man."

Fifteen minutes later, on the computer in Asher Glick's office next to the bedroom, Flack found a file of all the jobs Glick had performed for the past five years, including the work he had done, the cost to him in time and material and the money paid for each job. Flack also found a file showing outstanding debts. One of those was for $42,000 owed by Arvin Bloom from the morning *minyan*. It was almost two months overdue.

In parentheses under the Bloom entry were the words "Time to face him."

Flack went through Glick's e-mail, focusing on the last two days. There were ads for Viagra, Cialis, Rolex watches, cruises to Alaska. Flack went to the "Saved" file, opened it, scrolled down until he came to a recent one from Glick to Bloom. The message read:

So you are my old Yeshiva school mate from Chicago. Welcome to New York. I'm sorry you have been ill, but I hope you are better now, at least well enough to see an old friend. Remember Chaver Schloct, how easy it was to

get the poor little man flustered? I wonder what hap-
pened to him. In any case, I'd like to see you again. It
would also be nice if you sent me a check for the money
you owe me for the 18th century English dining room
table and eight matching chairs your wife purchased from
me. Partial payment would be fine for now. This financial
transaction however has nothing to do with my desire to
see you.

Asher Glick

Chad Willingham looked up from the microscope, rubbed his head, making him look even more like Stan Laurel, and grinned at Aiden.

"Minute, minute, minute please," he said, moving to the nearby computer and Googling the page he was searching for. "There."

He pointed to the web page, which showed what looked like a panel of dark wood at the top.

"Bloodwood," he said. "Great name. Grown in Brazil, French Guiana, Suriname."

"Rare?" she asked.

"Think so," he said. "Durable stuff, used for flooring, cabinets, furniture. Ever tried broiled iguana?"

"This have something to do with bloodwood?" asked Aiden.

"Not that I know of," he said. "There's just a place in Chinatown that serves it."

"You asking me to go to dinner with you to eat an iguana?"

"No," he said. "I just thought it was interesting, like seeing a unicorn."

"A unicorn," Aiden said skeptically.

"You know the James Thurber story?" he asked. "The one in which the man sees a unicorn in his garden and goes inside to tell his wife and she says he's a booby and she's putting him in a booby hatch, only she's the one who winds up in the booby hatch?"

"Is there a point to this, Chad?"

"I like finding unicorns," he said with a grin.

The reasons for supporting the use of virtual autopsy were many, but the primary times Hawkes had used it were on members of the traditional Jewish faith. The procedure involved computer topography and magnetic resonance imaging. The procedure could also accurately determine the time of death using Virtopsy, MRI spectroscopy. When the procedure is used, a 3-D portrait of the corpse appears on a computer screen. The device can measure metabolites in the brain that emerge during post-mortem decomposition.

The primary reason not to use Virtopsy was that few courts were inclined to accept the results. As a witness, Hawkes had always come to the point in the questioning by the defense attorney where he was asked if he had actually seen the organs. In this case involving an Orthodox Jew, the defense would have to be told that a Virtopsy was performed.

A decent defense attorney would almost certainly ask if Dr. Hawkes thought the results from Virtopsy were as thorough as those in the far more accepted standard autopsy.

"It would depend on who performed the procedure," Hawkes would say.

Then it would come. The defense attorney would ask: "Do you think this virtual autopsy was as thorough as you would have done in your standard autopsy?"

And Sheldon Hawkes would be forced to say, "No."

Hawkes had decided to do his best to respect the wishes of Asher Glick and his religion, but when it came down to Hawkes looking at the very white naked man on the table in front of him, he reached for his long forceps. Even if he had to be intrusive, he would at least be able to say that he had tried. He had the information from the Virtopsy. He could focus on what the procedure had revealed. Three years earlier, Hawkes had been reamed by the deputy police commissioner for the bloody autopsy he had performed on a man named Samson Hoffman, who turned out to be an Orthodox rabbi, a singular fact that no one had bothered to share with Hawkes.

So, now he began on Asher Glick by carefully removing the two bullets lodged in his brain. The Virtopsy had revealed their location. They came out cleanly, in good shape. He dropped the bullets in a metal bowl.

Normally, he would simply cut across the corpse's chest from shoulder to shoulder and then saw down the center of the rib cage. This would be followed by pulling back the ribs like two reluctant doors, beyond which were the vital organs. Instead, it took Hawkes about two hours to do this autopsy, being as careful and minimally intrusive as possible.

He had three more corpses waiting for him, and who knew how many more might come in while he sat waiting?

Hawkes was tired: sixteen hours without sleep, too much coffee, a badly burned corpse early that morning. He had discovered that she had been strangled before she was burned.

When he was finished with Glick, he returned the man's body to the drawer from which it had come, opened another drawer and moved the corpse of Eve Vorhees to the just-scrubbed steel table. She was a good-looking woman with neatly trimmed dark hair and punctured with holes.

From time to time he had heard the comment at funerals that the corpse looked "peaceful." Usually, that look had been manipulated by someone at the funeral home.

This one, Hawkes thought, looking at the woman, looks genuinely at peace.

He plugged the earpiece of his iPod into his right ear, put the iPod in his chest pocket and turned it on. It was a day for 1950s modern jazz, the plaintive trombones of J.J. Johnson and Kai Winding, the deep soulful sounds of Gerry Mulligan's sax and the sad knowing voice of Chet Baker singing *You Don't Know What Love Is*.

When Hawkes made the first incision he was unaware that he was singing along with Baker.

The photographs were laid out on the clean laboratory table along with a small stack of computer printouts. Stella waited while Aiden took a white plastic bottle of saline solution from the drawer, tilted her head back and let two drops fall into each eye.

Stella knew that looking at the computer screen for hours took its toll. Two years earlier, Matt Heath, a twenty-one-year-old computer geek with a winning smile and uncontrollable red hair, had finished a sixteen-hour shift at the computer. When he tried to get up, he was dazed, his vision blurred, and he had fallen to the ground with a seizure and gotten a split head that took ten stitches.

He had come back to work after three days, wearing thick glasses. He seemed to be his old self until he sat down in front of the screen. He turned on the computer, listened to it hum to life, desktop images appearing against a light blue background. Matt Heath had immediately turned off the computer, gotten up and walked out the door. Stella heard he was now attending a gourmet cooking school in Zurich.

"You okay?" asked Stella.

"Fine," Aiden said, picking up the printout and handing it to Stella. "Look what we've got."

"What time's your appointment?" Mac said, looking over Danny's shoulder at the computer screen.

"Two," said Danny.

Mac had ordered Danny to make the appointment with Sheila Hellyer, the on-call NYPD psychologist. Everyone had periodic evaluative sessions, usually very short, with Sheila or one of the other psychologists.

Mac had gone through five sessions with her after Claire died on 9/11. It had helped. He looked down at Danny's hands on the keyboard. The tremor in the right hand was definitely there, but Danny managed to type, sometimes having to delete things and go back over keys.

Mac didn't have a tremor after Claire's death. He had a sudden pronounced tic of his right cheek. It wasn't something he could hide. He had taken time off and seen Sheila Hellyer. The tic had gone, but its disappearance had caused him to feel a constant guilt. While it made no sense, Mac felt that the tic was a reminder, maybe even a punishment, not just for his wife's death, but for the vanished guilt. There were times when he missed the comfort of that affliction.

A little more than a year earlier, Danny had been through a psychological evaluation after he had shot and killed a murderer who was shooting at him. At first Danny had simply seemed slightly distracted after the shooting. Gradually, he had begun to go into distant, dazed states for a minute or so. After the evaluation, Danny had gradually returned to his usual self, though the smile he had so often displayed appeared less and less.

"Fingerprints all over the crime scene," Danny said. "Most are what you'd expect, father, mother, daughter. Other ones, two in blood on the bed, look like a kid's, but we have no prints on record for Jacob Vorhees, though prints in his room do match. But there are some other very interesting ones."

"Kyle Shelton," said Mac.

"His prints are all over the daughter's room," said Danny. "Some of them in blood."

"We have an address?" asked Mac.

"Yeah. Should we get a pickup order out for him?"

Mac looked at his wristwatch and said, "I'll go on my own. You make it to your appointment with Sheila Hellyer."

Danny nodded, resigned.

*   *   *

Joshua sat erect, a compact black leather Bible open in his hands. His black suit and white shirt were without wrinkles, recently cleaned. He wore no tie and was freshly shaved. He looked up over reading glasses when Aiden and Stella entered the room. He had been waiting for them.

The two women sat across from him. Joshua closed the book and put it in his jacket pocket.

Aiden put the printout on the table. Joshua didn't look at it.

"Your shoes had sawdust on them," said Stella. "The sawdust matches the dust at the murder scene."

"Aren't you supposed to tell me now that I can have a lawyer?" he asked.

"You're not under arrest," said Stella. "But if you want a lawyer . . ."

Joshua shook his head "no."

"I was there yesterday," he said. "I went into that room and left a message on the wall: 'Christ is King of the Jews.' I did not criminally trespass. The doors to the synagogue were open. It is a house of worship. I did not deface property. The paint I used is easily washed off."

"Then let's try harassment," said Aiden.

"I welcome it," said Joshua. "A reprimand from a judge. Publicity for our beliefs. There is an evil among us, the devil. 'Be sober. Be vigilant; because your adversary the devil, as a roaring lion, walks about, seeing whom he may devour.' I Peter. Chapter five. Verse seven."

"Verse eight," said Stella.

Joshua looked up. Their eyes met. He took the Bible from his pocket, flipped through the pages, found what he was looking for and said, "Verse eight."

"When you read it almost every day, you don't forget," said Stella.

"Nuns, priests?" Joshua asked, his voice betraying a slight quiver as he wondered who had influenced her.

Stella didn't answer. There were lots of things Stella didn't forget. She had been one year old when she went into the city institute for orphans. When she was old enough, she was told that her father had abandoned her mother and his newborn baby and gone back to Greece, where he died in a knife fight in a bar. Stella's mother died of pneumonia and the state had taken the baby.

As she grew older she spent most of her time in the library, reading and watching movies. It was not nuns who had made her read both the Old and New Testament over and over. It was Stella herself.

Some of the air of confidence had seeped out of Joshua as he returned the book to his pocket. For an instant he looked like a boy, a frightened boy braving it out. Stella nodded at Aiden, who looked down at the report in front of her.

"Your name is not Joshua. It's Warner Peavey," Aiden said. "Your father wasn't a rabbi. He was a Baptist minister in Rock Island, Illinois. You're not even Jewish. As Warner Peavey, you do have three arrests on record. Did two years in Attica for armed robbery."

"I am Jewish," Joshua insisted. "I converted to Reform Judaism and then to Messianic Judaism. Most Messianic congregations don't believe you can be a Jew for Jesus unless you are born Jewish. Like Jesus, I was shunned by my faith. Did you know that anyone with Jewish parents is given the right to return to Israel as a citizen, even atheists and humanists, but not us? So here I am and here I and my congregation will grow in the heart of Crown Heights, and within these walls and in Yeshua's eyes, I am a rabbi."

"Circumcised?" asked Stella dryly.

"We don't require that," said Joshua. "All those things you have written there are the darkness of Warner Peavey. He was reborn five years ago as the person you see before you, Joshua, second to Moses; he who led the Israelites into the promised land when God told Moses he couldn't enter. It was Joshua who fought and defeated the armies of the people in the promised land. Joshua who brought down the walls of Jericho."

"You own a gun?" asked Stella flatly.

"No," said Joshua.

"You're left-handed," said Aiden.

"Yes," said Joshua.

Stella pushed a photograph in front of him. It showed the left side of Asher Glick's body and the chalk outline. Joshua looked at it and shrugged.

"Look at the chalk marks," said Stella.

Joshua looked down again and then up.

"The crucifix is not one continuous line," said Stella. "The killer paused every three feet or so. See how the chalk line is less heavy and tails off slightly to the left?"

"No," said Joshua.

"The nails," said Stella. "They're through the hands and feet and deep into the hard wood. I hammered a nail in. I didn't get it very deep and I wasn't going through flesh. It took someone strong to drive them in like that."

Joshua was mute.

"And," said Stella, "the medical examiner called us just before we came down here. The nails were driven in at a slight angle from left to right."

Joshua waited.

"So the killer was left-handed," said Joshua. "So are millions. So was Christ. I can show you proof in the Bible."

"Medical examiner also said whoever shot Glick knew what he was doing," said Aiden. "Two shots from behind, perfectly placed, like an assassination."

"Proving?" Joshua asked.

Stella looked down at the sheet in front of her and said, "You've had a busy life."

Joshua shrugged.

"When you left your parents, you did time for holding up a convenience store," she said.

"I was falling," Joshua said. "Like so many of the saints, I had to go to the depths before I raised myself up with the help of the Lord. How can one expect salvation without experiencing sin?"

"Your congregation knows you were in prison?" asked Aiden.

"Yes."

"When you got out," said Stella, "you became an apprentice to a carpenter."

"Humbly in the footsteps of Jesus, who never renounced his Jewish identity," said Joshua.

"Then," Stella continued, "you joined a Messianic temple."

"A gathering of the timid, the cowardly," said Joshua. "They didn't even turn the other cheek. They never stood up to let the first cheek be struck. I left them and started my own congregation."

Joshua looked at the two women and shook his head.

"I know how to fire a gun," he said. "I know how to wield a hammer and drive a nail. I am left-handed. But I did not kill Asher Glick. We believe in converting, convincing, not killing. If we kill, our cause is set back by years, decades."

"Look at this photograph," Aiden said.

He took it. It was the wall of the synagogue library on which was written CHRIST IS KING OF THE JEWS. He handed it back to Aiden.

"That's what you believe, isn't it?" Aiden pressed.

"Yes," said Joshua. "Is there anything else you wish to say to me?"

"That you're free to go," said Stella, "but we'll be talking to you again."

4

SHELDON HAWKES, listening to Dinah Washington singing *Love for Sale*, made the first incision into the naked corpse of Becky Vorhees after examining all the wounds in the girl's body, six in her chest and stomach, one in her neck. He reported the wounds, including the location, size and shape of each penetration, and the depth of each thrust of the knife, into the microphone above his head, which was attached to a recorder on a table nearby. He also recorded that, while there were signs of slight bruising and shallow penetration, she did not appear to have been raped.

There were many possible reasons and, if asked, he would give them, but he was sure Mac would have his own thoughts on the reason for the lack of deep penetration. Three would be obvious. One, the rapist had changed his mind. Unlikely given the violence of the attack. Two, the girl had fought him off. Three, the girl had not fought him off, but the rape had been interrupted.

The girl's mother had been stabbed five times, four times in the stomach and once in the chest, a deep hard thrust that broke through bone to the heart. There were no signs of recent sexual activity on the woman.

Finally, almost two hours later, Hawkes had the last body on the table. Howard Vorhees was a big man, more than two hundred pounds, in good shape, obviously worked out. He had been stabbed once in the back and twice in the stomach. Besides these wounds, the only other thing Hawkes found of possible interest was a purple bruising just above the man's right wrist. The bone beneath the bruise was not broken. If he were still alive, Vorhees would have been in pain.

"The blood from the victims has been typed and the DNA is being determined," Hawkes said into the microphone. "Assuming the wounds were all made by the same weapon, which I believe is likely, a determination will be made to conclude from the layering of the blood the order in which the victims were killed."

Hawkes flipped off the tape recorder and looked down at the dead man. If he could see the knife, he'd be able to confirm what he suspected.

For now, however, he could determine the order

in which the three members of the Vorhees family had been killed. For example, if the blood in the wounds of Becky Vorhees was hers alone with no traces of blood from any other family member, then she had almost certainly been murdered first. If the blood in the wounds of Howard Vorhees contained both his blood and that of his daughter but not his wife's, then he had been killed second. Once he had the blood reports, he would know with certainty.

He looked down at the placid pale face of Howard Vorhees. Hawkes had listened to sixteen Dinah Washington songs. The last, *Destination Moon*, was just ending.

Long before the days of the iPod, Hawkes had listened to Maxine Tucker, Sarah Vaughn, Dinah Washington over and over again. On one of those days, Hawkes had been sewing up a skeletal homeless man with a liver that looked like bulbous gray silly putty when a new body was wheeled in.

"Put it over there," he had told the paramedics, pointing to his left without looking up as he finished sewing the cavity closed.

After putting the corpse back in its assigned drawer, Hawkes had put a CD in his stereo and turned to the body that had been brought in moments earlier.

Behind him came the bittersweet voice of Maxine Tucker singing, "I wonder if it's worth the dyin.' " And in front of him lay the body of Maxine Tucker.

Hawkes had stood silently listening until the end of the song.

Hawkes sat next to Mac at the counter at Metrano's. Mac had coffee. Hawkes ate a gyro sandwich.

"Well?" asked Hawkes, reaching for a large glass of Coke.

"I think you're right," said Mac. "The girl was killed first. Then the mother. Mother's blood in her wound was over hers. The father was killed last."

"Makes no sense," said Hawkes. "You have three people to kill. The one you go after first is the one most likely to cause you trouble, the father, but he was last."

"Maybe he came into the girl's room after she and her mother had been stabbed," said Mac.

"He didn't hear all the noise?" asked Hawkes. "He wasn't taking sleeping pills or any other drug. I would have found traces in his stomach. Nothing wrong with his hearing that I could see."

"So," said Mac. "What was he doing when his wife and daughter were murdered?"

Hawkes shrugged.

"And why were the women laid out on the bed but the father was crumpled on the floor?"

Mac was looking into the tan depths of the coffee in his mug. Hawkes looked at him.

"You have an idea?" said Hawkes.

Mac nodded.

"You know where the boy's body is?" asked Hawkes.

"Maybe," said Mac. "I need to find Kyle Shelton."

"The Beast," said Hawkes. "It would also help if you could find the knife."

"We're working on that," said Mac.

Mac didn't like what he was thinking. Didn't like it at all.

Danny sat in the chair across from Sheila Hellyer. Her office was small, clean, as identified by polished wood as the CSI lab was identified by shining steel.

Sheila Hellyer was somewhere in her forties, good looking, classy, short gray hair, every strand in place, large silver earrings.

"Hold up your hand," she said.

He did. The tremor was there. Sheila Hellyer wrote something on the yellow lined pad in front of her.

"When did it start?" she asked.

"Noticed it this morning when I got up," Danny said, trying not to look uncomfortable.

"What did you think had happened?" she asked.

"My grandfather had Parkinson's."

"It come on him suddenly?" she asked.

"No, a little at a time according to my mother," he said.

"I don't think you have Parkinson's, but we'll run neurological tests."

"You've seen this before?" Danny said.

"Many times," she said. "Sometimes a tremor, a tic, a slurring of words and uncontrollable blinking of the eyes. It comes with the job. This happened to you once before."

Danny looked puzzled and said, "No."

Sheila Hellyer flipped through the papers in the folder, found the one she was looking for and said, "Two years ago you underwent a mandatory psych evaluation," she said. "You had shot and killed an armed murderer on a subway platform."

She put down the evaluation and said, "The recommendation was that you be allowed to go back to work, but that you should be evaluated every six months."

"I have been," Danny said.

"I know. It says here that in each evaluation session you showed some signs of resentment toward the evaluator."

"Maybe they were paranoid," said Danny seriously. "Stress of the job. I think one of the evaluators, Dr. Dawzwitz, had a tick in his right eye."

Sheila couldn't hold back the smile. He was right. He was also deflecting.

"I mentioned the tremor in your hand," she said.

"In your initial evaluation, Dr. Dawzwitz noted a small tremor in your right hand."

"No," protested Danny, trying to remember.

There had been so much to think about, so much not to think about. He had wanted to go to bed and pull the blanket over his head. He had also wanted to plunge into work, all-consuming twenty-four-hour work. Had his hand really trembled?

"What happened last night?" she asked.

Danny shrugged.

"When you held up your hand I could see your knuckles were bruised. I think one of them might be broken."

Danny looked away, sighed, examined his hand and said, "Two men tried to mug me last night on the way home from work."

"On the street?"

"Subway."

"And you were afraid?" she asked.

Danny smiled, a bitter smile.

"No," he said. "That was the problem. There were two of them. One had a knife. One had a lead pipe. I think I was happy to see them."

"What did you do?" she asked.

"Lost it," he confessed. "Beat the hell out of them. I heard a rib crack, a nose break, saw blood spurting. I kept punching. I wanted to kill them. I think I shouted or grunted or something."

"What were you thinking?" she asked.

"Thinking?" he said. "Nothing. I was seeing. Maggots. A dead little girl. A killer who wanted sympathy. And then more bodies, mangled, torn, sometimes faceless. An old woman dead on the floor of a subway car clutching her shopping bag. I thought I had forgotten most of them."

"And the man you killed two years ago, did you see him?"

"No," he said.

"You kept punching the two men on the subway after you had subdued them?" she asked.

Danny nodded.

"How did it feel?" she asked.

"Losing it? Scary. When I stopped punching and looked down at the two of them groaning, I didn't remember beating them. But maybe what was worse was that, scary as it was, I felt good about it."

"You don't get to touch the bad guys in CSI," she said.

"No. Not if we can help it. Even when we use force when we have to, it always winds up as an issue in court if there's a trial."

"This time you did use force," she said. "For all the victims you've seen, all the killers of the innocent you had to endure. You did something."

"The wrong thing," he said.

"And you regret it?" she asked.

"No," he said. "I let them go."

He looked down at his trembling hand and then up at her and said, "I just want the tremor to stop."

"I'll call Dr. Pargrave in neurology to set up tests and prescribe blood work," she said, making a note, "and I'll ask him to give you a prescription for propranolol for the tremors and a mild drug prescribed for combat veterans. Make an appointment with me for one week from today. If you need me sooner, call day or night." She handed him a card.

"What's wrong with me?" asked Danny.

"How much coffee do you drink on an average day?" she asked.

"Not much. Four, five cups."

"Cola?"

"Diet, three a day maybe."

"Too much caffeine. Cut the caffeine. Cold turkey."

Danny looked at her, adjusted his glasses and repeated, "What's wrong with me?"

Sheila Hellyer nodded and said, "Cop trauma. You've seen too much darkness, death. You hold it in and then, in your case, something triggers all the memories and you explode. That hand is angry."

"You sure I'll be OK?"

"No," she said. "That's why we're running tests. The tremor might get worse without the caffeine. What you should do is go home for a few days and meditate or rent all six *Star Wars* movies."

"Are you going to recommend that I be taken off the unit?" he asked.

Sheila Hellyer closed the file in front of her and said, "If I recommended that all of the walking wounded police officers be fired, the New York police department would probably be reduced to a few hundred people. Besides, a lot of those officers living with the horror of what they see and do are the best this city or any city has. Just my opinion. I'm not planning to write a paper about it."

The Stalker entered Stella's apartment using a copy of the key he had made himself from the one he had found in a drawer in the kitchen the first time he had been there. The first time he had picked the lock. It hadn't been easy. It wasn't something he knew how to do, but he had practiced at it, especially with the lock Stella had installed. He had purchased a lock just like hers, read a book on how to pick a lock, bought the right tools, and practiced.

It had taken him almost twenty minutes that first time he had entered Stella's apartment, and by the time he was finished he had been drenched in sweat from the fear of someone seeing him. He had also been afraid that he had left small scratch marks that she might notice.

Now was the third time he had been in her apartment, and this time he didn't bother searching drawers and accessing Stella's computer. It took too much time to put everything back exactly as it was so she wouldn't notice anyone had been there.

He moved quickly to the bathroom and opened the medicine cabinet. He knew where the bottle was. He took the bottle he had brought with him from his pocket and carefully, over the sink, poured the white-brown gel from the bottle he had brought into Stella's medication and shook Stella's bottle for a full two minutes.

He had learned how to make the gel, which used simple fly strips and turpentine, from notes he found on a bookmarked web site on her computer.

He had been certain it would work. The person who had written the notes knew about such things, but just in case, the man had tried the poison on a dozen white rats he had purchased at a pet show. He had told the woman who sold the rats to him that he was feeding them to his two corn snakes. The rats had died almost instantly. That wasn't good. He moved on to guinea pigs and finally a rhesus macaque monkey, tried various mixtures, percentages, until he found one that made the monkey immobile for about two minutes before it died.

She might take it that night. It might be days or weeks before she would need it, but she would need it. When she did take it, it would kill her quickly, but she would suffer.

He carefully cleaned and dried the sink using toilet paper and a spray bottle of cleanser Stella kept under the sink. He flushed the paper down the toilet, made sure it was gone, pocketed the bottle he had brought with him and returned Stella's half-full bottle of antihistamine syrup to the cabinet with the label facing out as he had found it.

Less than a minute later, he left the apartment. He would return when the time came. He wanted to be there when she died. He wanted her to live long enough to know why this was happening to her, but he would settle for simply knowing that she was dead.

Mac had returned just before dawn to the wooded area where Jacob Vorhees' bicycle and clothes were found. He wanted to use an ALS on the area to look for signs of blood. With his luminol light on and wearing an amber eye-shield, Mac went over the ground, moving outward in circles to a distance of fifty yards.

No signs of blood, but as dawn came, Mac found the missing sneaker behind a rock, half a football field away from the bike and clothes. Had the boy broken away from Kyle Shelton still wearing one shoe? Had the shoe come off when the boy was running away?

Wearing latex gloves, Mac lifted the shoe and saw the blood. He bagged the shoe and put it in his kit.

Mac had a few ideas. Some were simple, some—one in particular—were bizarre, but he had dealt with more than the bizarre before.

There were at least six linden trees in the area Mac covered. He had examined leaves from beneath some of them. Most of them had the edges gnawed off or an irregularly shaped hole in the middle of the leaf. It didn't take much searching to find silken threads on the trees and then cankerworm larvae on the still-living leaves of the linden tree.

Magnified 120 times and focused, the leaves revealed two secrets.

There was one small bite mark at the edge of one leaf near the stem. There was also a trace of something else, something white and pulpy. Mac increased the magnification until he was convinced the small white dot was animal material, almost certainly from a dead caterpillar very much like the one he had found on the linden leaf in Jacob Vorhees' room.

Back in his office, Mac checked his watch. He had a busy morning ahead. He sat back in his office chair and looked down at the two items on his desk, the fragment of leaf and a credit card printout, items related to the murder of the Vorhees family.

When Danny came through the door holding a folder and a book, Mac didn't look at his hand or ask him any questions about his session with Sheila Hellyer. Instead he asked, "What do we know about Kyle Shelton?"

Danny opened the folder and scanned the report. He already knew what was in it.

"Age twenty-five, degree from City University of New York, in philosophy. Did three years in the marines, enlisted. Served on the Iraq-Syria border. Purple heart. Punctured spleen from a mine. Got out, took a job delivering flowers. Had a fight in a bar on the Lower East Side, The Red Lamp Lounge. Some guy, a little drunk maybe, got in Shelton's face about Middle East policy. Shelton shut him up by breaking the guy's jaw with one punch. Shelton spent three months at Riker's and then got a hearing and was given probation. And last, but maybe not least, our fleeing Beast wrote a book, *War and Rationalization*. Published by a respectable small press. Got a short favorable review in the *Times* on a Tuesday. The book didn't sell, only two thousand copies."

Danny handed Mac a copy of the thin book. Mac opened it to the inside back flap and saw the face of a serious young man looking back over his shoulder at the camera.

Early that morning, before he went to the woods just before the sun rose, Mac, warrant in hand, had gone to Shelton's studio apartment in a gray, uninviting prewar stone building. He had found lots of Shelton's prints. He felt certain they matched the bloody ones at the Vorhees house.

Shelton's room was clean, dominated by a

gleaming all-purpose exercise machine. One solid dark wood bookcase was filled with books, mostly about philosophy and psychology: Jung, Freud, Nietzsche, Sartre, some names Mac didn't recognize. The bottom shelf was filled with CDs. Shelton's taste, like Mac's, ran to the Baroque: Bach, Vivaldi, Hayden, Mozart. There was a slightly faded futon against the wall across from two windows, which had recently been cleaned. A heavy dark wood chest with six drawers rested against the wall. A round well-polished wooden table with two metal folding chairs stood next to the refrigerator and built-in pantry. A small desk with a chair stood against the last wall. A computer, slightly past its prime, sat on the desk. Mac checked the computer files and e-mail.

The Beast was a puzzle. He received and sent e-mails about the need for a massive movement to send troops or mercenaries into lawless African countries. He was ready to go fully armed and ready to kill if a mercenary army could be organized. He also received and sent e-mails about children starving and dying in third world countries, and abuse of children in all countries. Some of the e-mails were clearly written in a rage. In all of his e-mails, Shelton quoted philosophers, novelists, poets and psychiatrists.

There had been no copy of Kyle Shelton's own book in his apartment.

"So," said Mac. "Shelton is smart."

"Looks that way," said Danny.

Mac looked at the credit card printout on his desk and said, "If he's so smart, why did he use his Visa card for gas a few hours ago in New Jersey?"

"No cash?" Danny guessed.

"He could have gotten cash from an ATM in Manhattan," said Mac.

"He wants us to know he was in New Jersey," said Danny. "He wants us to think he's running west or north. Or he could also be doubling back and heading south."

Mac nodded his agreement, his eyes on the credit card statement.

"My guess is that he's on the way back here," said Mac. "Probably here already. There's something he has left to do."

When Danny left, Mac removed the leaf from the sealed see-through bag and twirled it by the stem.

You have something important to tell me, Mac thought. *But what?*

A second check of the Vorhees neighborhood turned up a single linden tree in the backyard of Bob and Shirley Straus.

Mac found the Strauses, who were in their early sixties, wearing shorts, broad-brimmed hats and loose-fitting long-sleeved shirts as they worked in their garden. The Strauses knew the Vorhees family casually, but they had never visited each other's homes or belonged to the same church or club. Bob Straus, who wiped his sweating neck with a red bandana, assumed the Vorhees' were Republicans, but he didn't know where he had gotten the idea. Had any of the Vorhees family been in the Straus backyard? Both Bob and Shirley said it was possible, but they didn't think so. No reason for them to.

Mac had walked over to the linden tree and picked a leaf up off the ground. It was a good match for the one he had taken from Jacob Vorhees' bedroom.

"We're going to save that tree," said Bob, pointing a trowel at the trunk.

"Inchworm infestation," Shirley said, pushing back the brim of her hat so she could get a better look at Mac. "Late in the year for it, too. Thank God it hasn't gotten to this neighborhood, but if it does come, we'll be ready for them."

To Mac she sounded like a feisty character from a horror movie saying she and Bob would be prepared when the zombies came ambling down the street.

"Think the worms will miss us," said Bob. "They only live a few weeks."

"And then there's something else," said Shirley.

Bob nodded in agreement and said, "Mites. But we've kept them from touching our trees.

"Trade-off," Bob continued, returning the bandana to his pocket. "We use chemicals. Maybe add a little pollution into the ground and air, but if we didn't, it would be the end of our trees."

When Mac turned to leave, Shirley Straus said, "Detective?"

Mac turned back to look at her.

"The boy," she said. "Jacob. Is he . . . ?"

"We don't know yet," said Mac.

"I can't . . ." she began.

Before she could cry, her husband was at her side, one arm around her shoulder.

"We have two boys, men now," said Bob Straus. "Can't imagine what it would be like . . . I hope he's alive."

His wife nodded in agreement, holding back tears.

"We'll find him," said Mac.

He didn't say whether he expected to find the boy dead or alive. Mac thanked them and drove back to the lab.

Arvin Bloom's furniture shop on Eighty-second Street just off of Second Avenue was small, but in a good location near dozens of antique shops, many specializing in furniture.

When Stella, Flack and Aiden entered, they could hear a soft buzzer sound in the rear of the shop and they could smell the mixture of new and old wood.

The shop was packed with furniture, large armoires, dressing tables, desks, a few ornate lamps and four huge crystal chandeliers overhead.

From an alcove a big balding man in his fifties with a paunch appeared, wearing a suit and carrying an apron, which he placed on a wooden armchair with a gold cushion. Stella was sure the cushion was both old and silk. The man walked slowly.

"Looking for something in particular?" the man asked with a smile.

Something about the smiling man irritated Flack, who took out his wallet, showed his shield and said, "Arvin Bloom? We're looking for a murderer."

Bloom looked at the two women, puzzled.

"I don't understand," he said.

"Asher Glick was murdered yesterday," said Flack.

Bloom bowed his head. "I know. I was going to sit *shiva*, but, to tell the truth, I don't know if I'd be welcome."

"Why not?" asked Stella.

"I owe Asher a great deal of money," he said.

"Forty-two thousand dollars," said Aiden. "We checked the business log on his computer."

"Actually, more than that," said Bloom. "My wife made the purchase from Asher. She saw it for the bargain it was and checked it with me. I was bedridden at the time. Prostate cancer. I'm fine now. Radiation treatment and radiation pellet implants. When Ivy, my wife, was talking to Asher, it turned out that we were Yeshiva students together."

"Can we speak to your wife?" asked Flack.

"Certainly," said Bloom. "I'll get her. Would you like some coffee? I always have it brewing for customers. Coffee and tea. Trade secret; if a potential customer accepts coffee, tea, wine, cookies, they feel obligated, not necessarily to buy, but to look more seriously than they might have done otherwise."

"I'll remember that," said Aiden.

"I will pay every penny I owed Asher to his family," Bloom said. "This is an up and down business. I have two pieces with buyers for the pieces we bought from him. They will bring in more than enough money to pay what I owe."

"Do you mind if I look around?" asked Aiden.

"Please do," said Bloom. "And feel free to ask any questions or touch any item as long as you are careful."

"I'll be as careful as I am with crime scene evidence," said Aiden, kit in hand, moving past Bloom, who followed her with his eyes.

"There's a small workspace back there where I make minor restorations myself," Bloom said. "My wife and I have an apartment up there." He indicated a wooden staircase that led up to a pair of doors.

Bloom looked at Stella and Flack, nodded, and said, "I'm a suspect, aren't I? The young lady said something about a crime scene."

"You're someone who might be able to supply us with some information," said Flack.

Stella moved to the chair where Bloom had dropped his apron. She opened her kit.

When she took out the mini vacuum, Bloom said, "I think you need my permission to do that."

"What do you think I'm going to do?" Stella asked.

"Vacuum my apron for evidence," Bloom said.

"You know about forensics?" said Flack.

"A little, television," said Bloom with a shrug. "Go ahead. Permission granted. But your time would be better spent looking for the lunatic who killed Asher."

"What lunatic?" asked Flack.

"Joshua," said Bloom. "He's a madman."

"You were part of the *minyan* yesterday," said Stella after she had carefully vacuumed the apron.

"You want to take it?" said Bloom. "Take it."

"Thank you," said Stella, carefully folding the apron and placing it in her kit.

"When was the last time before yesterday that you were part of a *minyan*?" asked Flack.

Bloom smiled.

"When I was fifteen," he said. "I had a bar mitz-vah when I was thirteen. I was considered a man who could make up the sacred number. A man named Ruben Goldenfarb found me on a street corner with some other kids. This was back in Cincinnati. He didn't ask me if I wanted to come. He simply said, 'Come,' and I came."

"Then why yesterday?" asked Flack.

"I had recovered from my treatment and I wanted to see Asher. He suggested I join the *minyan* and we could talk afterward. I said yes. I owed him. More than money. He was good to me, steered buyers to me."

"We know," said Stella. "We were at Mr. Glick's store."

"Your wife," said Flack, reminding the man that they wanted to talk to her.

As if on cue, one of the doors at the top of the landing opened and a woman came down the steps. She was short, slightly overweight, wearing a colorful orange and yellow dress. Her hair was short, touches of gray, neatly brushed, and she was wearing makeup and no smile. Aiden pegged her at forty plus.

"My wife," said Bloom with a smile. "These are the police. They want to ask you some questions about Asher Glick."

The woman vaguely registered Bloom's words and took a few seconds to turn her head to look at him, then turned to look at each of the strangers before her.

"He's dead," she said softly.

"When did you last see him?" asked Stella.

"I only saw him three times," she said. "Always at his shop to look at merchandise. The last time was, I think, last Monday. We bought a French Regency period commode, early nineteenth century, three doors, carved walnut with a marble top from L'île-de-France."

"It didn't have the original hardware," said Bloom, "but Ivy knew that I had perfect period hardware. And the legs needed a little work. The restoration is undetectable. It is one of the pieces we have a buyer for."

"Your computer," Flack prodded.

"My accounts," answered Bloom. "I prefer the old-fashioned way, the feel and smell and touch of a craftsman's shop."

Bloom moved behind the counter, reached down to a shelf and pulled out an oversized old clothbound notebook.

"Before I forget," said Bloom, making some notes in the book with a pen he pulled out of a white mug on the counter. "I keep track of where I am on each job."

"We checked Mr. Glick's computer," said Stella.

"Yes?" said Bloom, looking up over the top of his glasses.

"What we didn't find on Mr. Glick's computer was more interesting," said Stella.

Bloom looked puzzled.

Aiden appeared from the back of the shop, nodded for Stella to follow her.

"We didn't find anything he bought or sold in the last year made of bloodwood," Stella said, nodding at Aiden. "There was nothing in his shop made of bloodwood. But Asher Glick had bloodwood dust on his clothes. Do you have anything made of bloodwood?"

"Yes, back where your friend was," said Bloom. "A beautiful piece. I was working on it when you came. My guess is that a fair number of people Asher was doing business with have pieces made of bloodwood. Have you checked them?"

"None of them were part of that *minyan*," said Stella. "None but you."

Stella left Flack with Bloom and joined Aiden in the small back room. Aiden pointed to a red sideboard.

"Transfer from Bloom to Glick," said Aiden. "Can we match sawdust to a specific piece of furniture?"

"I don't know," said Stella, "but we're going to find out."

"He's not left-handed," said Flack as they left the shop.

Neither Aiden nor Stella responded. They had

both noticed the same thing. Wristwatch on Bloom's left wrist. Notes he made in his notebook with his right hand. The killer's chalk marks, hammered nails, and written message near the body were definitely made by a left hand.

"But he avoided telling us if he had a computer," said Stella. "We know he does."

"Glick's e-mail," said Aiden. "He sent messages to Bloom."

"Could use a computer at the library or an Internet coffee bar," said Flack.

"Could be," Stella said. "Let's find out if he's got one."

"Will do," said Flack, wondering what they would find on Bloom's computer when he found it—and Flack was sure he would find it.

Kyle Shelton had abandoned the pickup on a street in the Bronx. The street, he knew, was an elephants' graveyard of abandoned cars. He didn't bother to wipe off fingerprints. He did bother to remove the license plate and tuck it into his backpack. It was four blocks to the subway station in a neighborhood where a white face was a rare exception.

In spite of the name on the vanity plate, Kyle Shelton's nickname was not The Beast. The plates had belonged to his cousin Ray, as had the pickup truck. People just assumed the nickname went with the driver. Kyle felt nothing about abandoning the pickup. It was a piece of crap, falling apart, rusting through the bottom, radio a spray of static, brakes needing fluid every two weeks. Ray wouldn't care either, but he would want his plates back.

Kyle hitched the pack onto his shoulders. It contained clothes, a disposable razor, a toothbrush, a few books, a few nutritional bars. It had two more items too. One of them was a long-bladed kitchen carving knife encrusted with dry blood. Kyle had considered throwing it away, but he decided to hold on to it. He didn't know much about forensic evidence, but he knew there were things Crime Scene Investigators could find that might help him with what he was trying to do.

It was midday, the sun burning bright in the clear sky, humidity coming thick from the air. He felt the moist itch in his crotch, under his jeans and against his scalp. It had been this hot in Iraq, especially on the unsafe roads across the desert, bouncing, hallucinatory.

The streets of the towns of Iraq had been dangerous for a soldier, more dangerous than this street in the Bronx.

The buildings on the street were mostly two- and three-story brick apartments built in the 1920s. Between some of them were debris-filled lots where buildings had been torn down.

Kyle had a plan. It wasn't much of a plan, but it was all he could come up with. He had slept in the pickup the night before for about two hours. He was tired. He half closed his eyes and was aware of children somewhere in the distance laughing and arguing. What he wasn't aware of until he heard the voice was the three young men standing on the crumbling stone steps of one of the old three-flat buildings Kyle was about to pass.

"You lost?" asked the voice.

Kyle looked up. The speaker was maybe eighteen or nineteen, black, hair cut short, clean yellow T-shirt and brown jeans. Flanking the speaker were two other young black men wearing identical T-shirts and brown jeans.

Kyle didn't answer. He pulled the brim of his baseball cap down, shifted the weight of his backpack and kept walking.

"Asked you a question, brother," said the young man, who was obviously the leader. There was irritation in his voice now.

Kyle stopped, tilted back his cap and looked at the young men who had taken a step toward him. He had been through situations like this, on the streets of Fallujah, at Riker's.

"Bo asked you a question," said the young man to the right of the leader.

" 'Life is not a spectacle or a feast. It's a predicament,' " said Kyle, reaching over his shoulder into his backpack.

"Say what?" asked Bo.

"George Santayana," said Kyle. "A philosopher."

"He's high," said one of the others.

"Hand over the backpack," said Bo, holding out his hand.

The three took another step toward Kyle, who shook his head "no."

" 'I believe in the brotherhood of all men, but I don't believe in wasting brotherhood on anyone who doesn't want to practice it with me. Brotherhood is a two-way street,' " said Kyle. "You know who said that?"

"Don't give a shit," said the young man.

The young man on the right pulled a small gun from his pocket after looking up and down the street to be sure no one was watching.

Kyle didn't seem to notice.

"Malcolm X," said Kyle. "He said it. You know who he was."

"I ain't simple," said the leader. "Saw the movie."

Kyle's right hand came out of the backpack holding a .45 caliber army pistol, which he aimed at the leader. The trio stopped.

"You gonna shoot all three of us?" Bo said.

"Looks that way," said Kyle. "Unless he puts that gun away and you all back up and sit down on the steps and talk about the heat and listen to the radio or some CDs."

The one called Bo scratched the side of his head, smiled and looked at Kyle.

"I like you," said Bo.

"That makes me very happy," said Kyle. "Adds to my new philosophy."

"What's that?" the leader said, still smiling.

" 'I'm only going to dread one day at a time,' " said Kyle.

"Who said that?" asked the leader.

"Charles Schulz," said Kyle.

"Who?" asked Bo.

"*Peanuts*," said Kyle.

"Crazy fool. Get out of here," said the leader, waving his hand.

Kyle nodded, put the gun back in his pack, and walked the rest of the way to the subway without looking back. He had things to do.

5

THE FIRST TIME, with Glick, he had made mistakes.
There was no point in deluding himself. He had
thought he was prepared, but he had let emotion
take over, something he had been taught never to
do. No, it wasn't really emotion moving him to the
kill, making him take chances. It was the high of
running along the edge when he could take a safe
path. It was the rush he got from pulling it off, and
so he had made it difficult for himself and those who
would be looking for him. He had something to
prove to himself. His plan had been weak. It was un-
professional. It could get him caught. It could get
him killed. He could, as he had almost done, lose
control of the situation. He had been out of the game
too long.

Yes, that was it. He comforted himself by saying
that it had been a long time since he had called on

his training, his skill. He hadn't really forgotten. He had put it aside for a new life.

It was early afternoon. His armpits were sweating and even he was aware of the odor. He wore a short-sleeved white shirt with a tie. The shirt was soaked through. The radio had said the temperature was about to top 100 degrees and the humidity wasn't far behind. He walked slowly, steadily.

No one paid attention to him or each other unless they were traveling together. He pulled the extra-long brim of his brown fedora farther down his forehead. The hat definitely did not go with the white shirt. Most people, if asked later, would only remember the hat that shaded the man's eyes. By the time the first witness mentioned the hat, it would be gone, burned to nothingness.

The well-worn briefcase in his hand was hefty but not really heavy. He had kept the contents minimal. He passed the storefront of the Jewish Light of Christ, glancing through the window without moving his head. His peripheral vision was excellent and well honed. He hadn't lost that and he knew from how he had handled the Glick killing that his hand was still steady and his aim nearly perfect.

He entered the narrow news shop, moved past the ATM, the counter behind which the cigarettes and cigars were neatly stacked, the refrigerator with glass windows behind which were lined-up soft drinks and prepackaged tuna salad, egg salad and chicken salad sandwiches. A machine on his right featured a Ferris wheel ride of skewered hot dogs and Polish sausages.

A short, lean man, about fifty, wearing an ugly, colorful shirt with dozens of different-colored stripes, stood behind the counter at the front of the shop. The man had glanced up at him, decided he was respectable, and returned to a newspaper in some foreign language.

He had been here before. Twice, making sure that on this, his third visit, the person behind the counter was different from the others, probably all members of the same Korean family. All Asians did not look alike to the man. He had spent years in Asia, Japan, both Koreas, Vietnam, Laos, Cambodia, Thailand.

The steel back door was closed. The last time he was here he had oiled the hinges to keep them quiet.

He went through the door, closing it behind him gently. He was in a narrow alleyway, garbage cans already overflowing, hearing the scurry of rats, the sound of horns and moving vehicles on the street muffled by the buildings.

He moved slowly to the door he had already checked. They had left it unlocked. They always did. They had nothing to steal but their faith.

He slipped on a pair of surgical gloves, stepped through the door, closing it behind him, and stood in the semidarkness of the small storage room, listening. He knew their routine. In a few minutes, they would all go out together to the park, kosher sandwiches in brown bags. They'd be gone a little less than an hour, eating, talking, listening to Joshua.

They always left someone behind. Someone to remain in the storefront synagogue, to be ready in case someone appeared to ask questions, to show interest.

He opened the door slightly, hoping it would not be a woman who was left behind. Yes, a woman would confuse the police, but it would also slightly change the pattern he wanted to establish. Luckily, it wasn't a woman. It was a thin, young man with a beard, dark slacks, a clean, neatly pressed short-sleeved off-white shirt. The young man's back was to the storage closet. He was absorbed in what he was reading. He had no sense of the person in the rubber-soled shoes who, leaning low, silently crept up behind him.

When he was no more than two feet behind the young man, he pressed the palm-sized .22 caliber semiautomatic Walther in his hand against the man's head and fired two hollow-point bullets, knowing the sounds of the street and the dying man's thick hair and skull would muffle the shot. The young man slumped forward, clinging to the book. The man pushed the body to the floor and looked out the window. He picked up the brass bullet casings and pocketed them.

Satisfied that no one was looking, he stepped over the body, moved quickly to the door to lock it. He swiftly dragged the corpse to the storage room. Once inside, he opened the briefcase he had left there, put the gun inside and took out a heavy hammer, four thick pointed bolts and a piece of white chalk.

Then he went back into the alley and through the door to the narrow magazine shop. He had something to tell the man behind the counter, something that would change his life.

"Possibilities?" asked Mac, a cup of machine-brewed cappuccino in his hand.

He was standing next to Danny Messer in the spotless chrome snack room with uncomfortable black plastic-covered chairs. Along one wall a battery of machines—sandwiches, candy, soft drinks, coffee—hummed and glowed colorfully. They were the only people in the room.

"Shelton killed the boy, buried the body," said Danny, working on a Diet Coke he held in his non-trembling hand. "We just haven't found it. Went over the ground where we found the clothes and bikes with probes, detection machines. Nothing."

"Maybe Shelton buried him somewhere else," said Mac.

"Why? He gets the kid to take off his clothes. Now he has a naked scared kid. Why not just kill him there and bury him?"

"Maybe the boy's not dead," said Mac.

Danny nodded. He had considered it.

"Shelton's hiding him somewhere?" asked Danny. "Pedophilia?"

"Nothing in his record that would suggest it," said Mac.

"The girl?" Danny tried.

"Hawkes says there are signs of recent sexual activity," said Mac. "Interrupted or stopped. Shallow penetration, no semen."

"Could still be sex," said Danny, taking a deep gulp, trying not to look at his hand.

"Could be," Mac agreed, "Or maybe he's into torturing children."

"Again," said Danny. "Nothing in his record to support that."

"Okay," said Mac. "That still leaves us with four questions. One, where are the boy's glasses? Two, why did I find the boy's single bloody shoe fifty yards from the crime scene? Three, why would Shelton kill the Vorhees family and lay the women out respectfully and leave the father in a twisted heap on the floor? And four, why kill the father last instead of first?"

"Want to play a video game?" asked Danny.

Mac shrugged, gulped down the last of his

nearly tasteless cappuccino. Mac knew that Danny was suggesting creating a virtual room on the computer in the lab. Danny finished his Diet Coke and dropped the empty bottle in the recycling bin.

The two men walked down the hall to the computer lab. There was no one else in the room. Danny moved to one of the computers, pressed a key and watched as the desktop images began to appear. Both men sat.

"I've got it programmed in," said Danny, controlling his right hand, which seemed to be somewhat better. He had taken the pills Dr. Pargrave had given him. They made him feel lightheaded, or maybe he just hadn't had enough sleep.

Danny moved the mouse to an icon marked VORHEES HOME and clicked. A photograph of the outside of the house appeared almost instantly. Danny hit another button and the image became a photograph of the foyer of the house, dominated by fresh white paint on the walls, a brightly lit, carpeted stairway to the left.

Using the mouse, Danny moved them up the stairs onto the upstairs landing and into the murder room. On the screen, the bodies of the two women were laid out on the bed, hands folded on their stomachs, eyes closed. The man was on the floor at the foot of the bed, contorted.

"Hawkes says the man had a badly bruised and cracked bone in his right arm," said Mac. "There's also a bruise, a cut and a cracked bone in his right cheek."

"Killer hit him," said Danny. "No blood on any object in the room that could have caused the blow."

"So," said Mac. "We may be looking for a killer with bruised knuckles."

Danny nodded.

"Finally, the knife wounds," Danny said, zooming in on the body.

"The knife wounds," Mac echoed. "The two women were stabbed, but not otherwise touched, except for the attempted penetration of the girl. Give me the room without the bodies and blood," said Mac.

Danny nodded, made the adjustments, and the girl's bedroom on the screen was now clean, the bed made, the blood gone, no bodies.

"Likely scenario?" asked Mac.

Danny moved the mouse, punched keys and a reasonable but not photographic likeness of the dead girl appeared on the screen. She was on the bed, clearly alive.

The door opened. A male figure stepped in. Danny hit more buttons on the keyboard and a knife appeared in the right hand of the male figure.

"Shelton?" said Danny.

"Why did he stop in the kitchen to get a knife?"

"He planned to kill her?" Danny asked, moving the figure across the room.

"Why come through the house?" asked Mac.

"He could have come through the window," said Mac. "It's not much of a climb."

The male image disappeared and suddenly the image on the screen was the side of the Vorhees' house. The male figure appeared at the window, opened it, climbed in and moved to the bed, where the image of the girl smiled up at him.

"The knife," Danny said. "If he came through the window, he'd have to go downstairs, get the knife and come back."

"Maybe he visited the girl regularly. She left the window open. He climbed in," said Danny.

"Let's play that one out," said Mac.

"Now," said Danny, working on the keys. "Mom hears them, comes in."

An image of Eve Vorhees came through the door, looked at the bed where there was now an image of her daughter on her back with the Shelton figure on top of her.

"Shelton panics," said Danny, manipulating the image. "Gets off the girl, kills her and then kills the shocked mother."

"And why kill the girl first?" asked Mac, looking at the screen, trying to come up with an alternative tale. "Hawkes says the wounds show he did. You'd think he would shut the mother up instead of continuing to stab the girl. The knife would have taken at least ten seconds to make those wounds, plenty of time for the mother to scream, rush out of the room."

"But she didn't run. He killed her next," said Danny.

"Where was the father?" asked Mac. "The odds are good that the mother or daughter would have started screaming."

The Shelton figure stabbed the girl, hurried toward the stunned wife, stabbed her and the door opened. A figure representing the father stood there, struck with horror. Before he can move, Shelton strikes.

"The stab in the back," Mac said.

The father figure, now with blood coming from his chest, turns, reaches for the door. The killer plunges the knife into the dying man's back.

"Won't play," said Mac. "The man's body was found at the foot of the bed. No blood by the door. He came all the way into the room."

Three dead figures on the screen. Danny manipulated the images and watched Shelton remove the knife from the dead man and place it in his belt. Then he laid the women out on the bed.

"The boy had to hear," said Mac.

No image of a boy appeared on the screen.

"Maybe," said Danny, "the boy heard, even opened the door, saw and ran for his bike. Shelton heard him and went after him."

"The boy was fully dressed at two in the morning?" asked Mac.

Danny shrugged and adjusted his glasses.

Mac sat silently, thinking about the knife, the problems with the scenario he had just witnessed, the leaf of the linden tree in the boy's bedroom, the leaf with the tiny bite marks of a cankerworm.

For more than an hour, in a small interrogation room, Flack talked individually to all of the nine people who had gone to lunch in the park. Many of them cried, not just the women.

One man, Morley Solomon, in his forties with curly white hair, a weathered face, and a deep white scar on his nose, said, "It's a test of our faith."

"By whom?" asked Flack.

"Perhaps Yeshua," said the man. "Some human instrument of his power, his dominion over the earth. A few will quit, but just a few."

"Not you," said Flack.

"No," said Solomon. "What proof is there of the power of one's beliefs unless those beliefs are tested? Like science."

"Science?"

"I used to be a physicist," said Solomon. "Princeton, theoretical research. I was a Jew. I remain a Jew. I will always be a Jew, but my faith will determine what a true Jew is, not the mandates and dictates of others. We observe the holy days, Rosh Hashanah, the Jewish New Year; Yom Kippur, the Day of Atonement; all of them."

There was only one person remaining to talk to.

Flack told everyone that they could go. All of them looked at Joshua, who nodded, smiled, made it clear that he would be all right.

"His name was Joel Besser," said Joshua in the interrogation room when the others were gone. "He was twenty-one years old."

As the others had said, Joshua confirmed that Joel had volunteered to stay behind only minutes before the others had left to have lunch in the park. Joshua also confirmed that Joel was more than liked. He was loved.

"He was murdered not for personality or spirit," said Joshua, "but because of what he represented."

"Which was?" asked Flack.

"Heresy in the eyes of the closed-minded and ignorant," said Joshua. "He was a Jew for Yeshua and that threatened people."

"People?" asked Flack.

"Need I say it?" said Joshua, closing his eyes. "The Orthodox, not two blocks from here."

"We'll look into it," said Flack.

"When can we have Joel's body?"

"Up to the medical examiner," said Flack. "Would you please pull your hair back from your forehead?"

Joshua complied.

There was a swollen and cut red bump at the man's hairline.

"When did you get that and how?" asked Flack, indicating that Joshua could release his hair.

"About an hour ago," said Joshua calmly. "I beat my head against the wall. You can see over there."

Flack turned and saw the indentation in the plaster board. He also saw what appeared to be a slash of blood.

"Why?" asked Flack.

"To show my grief over our loss," Joshua said. "The congregants watched and wept. When one of our people die, we want to share their pain. The Orthodox tear their clothes.

"We are Jews," Joshua said, his voice starting to rise, "Jews who suffer from discrimination by other Jewish denominations and by Christians."

"Where were you when Joel Basser was murdered?" Flack asked.

Joshua smiled knowingly and said nothing.

"Every person in your congregation says you left after five minutes in the park and didn't come back till it was time to head back to the synagogue."

"I left Morley Solomon in charge to talk about Einstein and the Messiah," said Joshua. "It's a passion of his."

"And where did you go?"

"A bar," said Joshua. "Babe Bryson's. You can ask the bartender. I was there for about forty-five minutes."

"Doing what?" asked Flack.

"Drinking," said Joshua. "I'm an alcoholic."

The well-worn wooden floor was decked with numbered red cones, which Aiden Burn had carefully placed around the chair where Joel Besser had been shot, as well as in a semi-regular line along each side of the continuous blood trail that led back to the storage room where the victim lay crucified on a cross drawn in chalk on the floor.

There was a single, creaking overhead fan turning slowly, producing nothing but noise. The smell of blood was warm and thick.

Aiden had taken photographs and blood samples and sprayed for fingerprints, although both she and Stella were reasonably sure the killer had worn gloves, an assumption supported by the fact that Aiden had found no prints on any of the four bolts driven into the dead man's hands and feet.

Stella leaned close to the body of the young man and used a Sirchie vacuum on his shirt, pants, arms. Back at the lab they would compare the photos of the chalk marks at each of the crucifixion murder scenes. Stella could already see that the marks were a match, but with a difference. These chalk marks were done more evenly, straighter.

The words in Hebrew were printed with much more care than at the earlier crime scene. The killer had taken some time.

As for the finger-thick nails through the dead man's palms and feet, they were much larger than those that had been used on Asher Glick. But they were driven in deeper. She had no doubt that Sheldon Hawkes would come to the same conclusion: the nails were driven in by someone using his left hand, someone powerful.

Aiden stepped into the storage room and looked around, taking more photographs. They had found no hammer, no extra nails. This time the killer had come prepared, brought his own tools.

Stella stood up and said, "He came through that door and went right up to Besser and shot him twice. Daylight. Windows uncovered. Could have been seen. Then he dragged the body back here. He picked a bad time and place to kill."

"Killing Glick and crucifying him in a synagogue on a weekday morning took time. That was a bad time and place to kill too, but he got away with it," said Aiden. "At least for now."

"He likes to take chances," said Stella. "Why?"

"Let's go back to the lab, wait for the ME's report and see what we've got," said Aiden.

Stella nodded her agreement.

The paramedics were parked on the street. The street was full of people of various colors, sizes and ethnic clothing. Aiden had taken photographs of the crowd. Not likely the killer would be out there, but she would check them against the photographs of the crowd outside the synagogue in which Asher Glick had been murdered.

Aiden knew it was possible that several innocent, curious people in the photographs were at both crime scenes. The murders had taken place only a few blocks from each other.

Aiden signaled to the paramedics, who came in with a body cart. She guided them around the cones to the small back room. One of the paramedics was a woman, black, pretty, no more than twenty-five. Her shoulders, arms and legs were well-muscled. The man was about the same age, white, big, strong.

They looked down at the body, showing no emotion as Stella said, "Leave the nails in the body. Move them as little as possible. Pry them up slowly. It's going to be a little tough. They're deep in the floor."

Both paramedics nodded. They had the tools and the experience and now they had a new story, one of the more interesting ones, something they could tell their family and friends.

" 'Sheep follow sheep,' " said the man, whose black-on-white plastic nameplate identified him as Abrams. He was looking down at the words written in chalk at the foot of the body.

All three women looked at him.

"That's what it says," said the man. "Hebrew. I think it's from the Talmud. He spelled sheep wrong."

*   *   *

The phone call came late in the afternoon while Mac was sitting alone going over the computer-generated crime scene images Danny had created, checking the Internet for information on linden trees and their parasites.

"Someone wants to talk to the CSI in charge of the Vorhees case," the lab tech who had taken the call said.

"Man?"

"Yes."

"And he said 'CSI'?" asked Mac, who was looking at the screen, where a pulpy white creature was inching its way along the rim of a heart-shaped leaf.

"Right," said the lab tech. "You taking it?"

"Put it through," said Mac. When he heard the click indicating an open line, he said, "Detective Taylor."

"Kyle Shelton," Shelton replied calmly.

Mac hit a button on the white phone carrier and put the phone back in its cradle. The call, now on speaker, was being automatically traced.

"What's on your mind?" asked Mac, who was busily going to the desktop file on the Vorhees case. He opened it and quickly found the pages on Kyle Shelton.

"You ever serve in the military?"

"Marines," said Mac.

"Me too," said Shelton, "but you know that."

"I know it," he agreed. "Is the boy alive?"

"Depends," said Shelton. "Life and death are transitions, a continuum."

"Is he alive?" Mac asked again.

"Yes," said Shelton wearily.

"You killed his family," said Mac.

" 'I am become Death, shatterer of worlds,' " said Shelton. "You know who said that? J. Robert Oppenheimer when he saw the first atomic explosion."

"You've been playing games with us," said Mac. "Why?"

"Games aren't over," said Shelton. "I have a present for you."

"What's that?"

"You've had time to trace this call," Shelton said. "Come here and find it."

"Shelton," Mac said.

"Sorry," said Shelton. "Out of time."

He hung up. Mac pressed a button and a voice answered.

"We've got it. We're on the way."

"Where?" asked Mac.

"He called from the Vorhees' house."

Flack sat back, his hands folded on the table, his head cocked slightly to the right. He was looking at Joshua and waiting.

"I'm not a fraud," said Joshua. "My mission is no small sordid cult."

"Do the others know about the drinking?" asked Flack.

"No," said Joshua. "I'm being tested by the Lord. Yeshua will show me the way."

"Meanwhile you have to have a drink during the day," said Flack.

"Yes," said Joshua with a sigh, "but I do not get drunk and I'm always lucid and focused."

"You kill Glick?" asked Flack.

"No."

"Joel Besser?"

"Why would I kill one of our own?" Joshua said incredulously.

"Divert suspicion," said Flack. "Or maybe he knew you killed Glick and was going to tell us."

The room was air-conditioned, but the air-conditioner was unable to function at full strength during a heat wave like this one. Flack knew from experience that there would be deaths from the heat, mostly old people living with open windows and unable to afford a fan, unable to get up, go down a flight of stairs or two and walk a block or more to an air-conditioned food market or a museum or the library. More people would die because of the suffocating heat than from murder.

"You have a devious mind," said Joshua.

"The job requires it," said Flack without emotion. He opened a file folder in front of him.

"And the murder of an innocent like Joel Besser

brings on the images I see waking and sleeping, the images that fade, but not completely, when I have a drink or two," said Joshua.

"Images?" asked Flack.

"Black babies, children," said Joshua, leaning forward. "Starving, ribs showing, leg bones without muscle, heads too large, pleading eyes too wide, beyond hope, mouths open, letting in flies. My faith is tested every moment of every day. Why would a benevolent God and His son allow this to happen? My mission is to understand. My weakness is that I am afraid the challenge is beyond my powers."

Joshua put his head in his hands, sobbed and said, "In a very real sense, I am responsible for the death of Joel Besser. I brought him into our fold with the promise of fellowship, a return to his abandoned Jewish identity and the hope of eternal life."

Joshua looked up at Flack, eyes wet, face slack.

"At times like this, I find it almost impossible to believe in those things. Do you believe in God? That there is a God?"

"Sometimes," said Flack, looking down at the file in the open folder. "You have any idea who might want to kill Joel Besser?"

"Yes," said Joshua.

"Let's talk about it and then check your hands for gun residue."

"Always a policeman," said Joshua, shaking his head.

"Always," said Flack.

The two uniformed officers at the Vorhees house had gone by the book. The problem was that the book changed every few years. A shrill sound was coming from a door across the entry hall. The two officers had gone to the door, weapons in hand, careful of where they were stepping in case there was trace evidence on the floor. The sound grew louder and more unpleasant with each step they took. The officer in the lead, Kitteridge, was young, broad shouldered, about thirty, a raspberry birthmark on his left cheek. The other officer, Nash, was overweight and probably close to retirement.

The younger officer pushed open the kitchen door. There was no one inside, but on the white table in the middle of the room was a telephone steadily giving off a low scream. As much as they wanted the noise to stop, they knew enough not to step into the kitchen and hang it up. The older officer closed the kitchen door and said, "Front, back?"

"Back."

The officers moved toward the front door, stepped outside and closed the door behind them. The sound of the screaming telephone disappeared. The younger officer moved quickly around the house to cover the back door.

"Nobody's been in, nobody out," Nash told Mac five minutes later. "We got here four minutes after you called it in."

Mac nodded, checked his watch. That meant thirty minutes had passed since the call from Shelton.

Mac put on a pair of latex gloves, shifted his kit to his left hand and took his gun from the holster on his belt with the right. Nash took out his service revolver again and followed Mac inside.

As he stepped forward, Mac noted, not for the first time, that the old house constantly spoke, with settling beams, creaking old floors and ceilings. The noisy air-conditioning had been turned off. Mac was sure he could still smell blood. He could also hear a familiar sound from the direction of the kitchen.

He moved forward, Nash at his side, weapon in hand, and pushed the kitchen door open. The four-chair white table was empty except for the white cordless phone that beeped to alert the owner that it was off the hook, the charger alongside it.

Mac moved forward and told Nash to call his partner inside. When Kitteridge came in, Mac said, "Check the house. Be careful. If you see or hear something suspicious, don't do anything. Just come back here and let me know. Don't touch anything."

"Right," said Nash.

The two officers moved past Mac and went through the door.

Mac moved to the kitchen table and looked around. Something wasn't right. He took out his camera and began taking pictures, ignoring the irritating screech of the phone.

When he was finished with the photographs, Mac dusted the phone for prints. The prints came up immediately. Mac photographed them and did a tape transfer before turning off the phone.

It rang almost immediately. Mac pressed the talk button and heard Shelton say, "Taylor?"

"Yes."

"I've been calling for the last ten minutes."

Mac said nothing. Shelton's game was on.

"I loved her," Shelton said after a long pause.

Mac detected the hint of a sob.

"Becky?" said Mac.

"Becky," Shelton confirmed. "Antoine de Saint-Exupéry wrote, 'Love does not consist of gazing at each other, but in looking together in the same direction.' You understand?"

"Yes," said Mac.

The kitchen door swung open and Nash stepped in.

"A knife," Nash said. "On the floor in the girl's bedroom. Looks like dried blood on it."

"I heard," said Shelton. "You found the knife. My fingerprints are on it, but it's really the weapon that tells the story."

"The ME will examine it carefully," said Mac.

"You want us to catch you but you don't want to make it easy."

"Something like that," said Shelton, "but not exactly."

"Want to tell me why you did it?" asked Mac.

"Not now," said Shelton.

Nash stood watching, listening, figuring out that Taylor was talking to the killer.

"The boy," said Mac.

"Had lunch today?" asked Shelton.

"No," said Mac.

"You might want a snack before you finish there," said Shelton. "I did."

"How about another quote?" asked Mac.

Mac doubted if Shelton could resist the request. The young man clung to the wisdom of others. He wasn't showing off his education or intellect. Mac was sure it was one of the few things that sustained him.

" 'The power of hiding ourselves from one another is mercifully given, for men are wild beasts, and would devour one another but for this protection.' "

"Nietzsche?" Mac guessed.

"Anne Frank," answered Shelton, who hung up. So did Mac. Mac opened his notebook and wrote down the quote. There was something wrong about it. An error? Mac put away his notebook.

Had Shelton mentioned lunch to avoid talking

about Jacob Vorhees? Probably, but it was more Shelton's style to deflect the question with a quotation. Mac looked around the kitchen, at the refrigerator, the cabinets, the door to the pantry, the white metal garbage can near the door. Mac moved to the can, stepped on the pedal and looked down at the contents of the fresh white plastic bag inside. It was empty. If Shelton had snacked before he left the house, he had either taken his trash with him or had eaten nothing that would leave trash. There was a third possibility. Shelton had lied about having a snack. But why?

Mac walked to the refrigerator and opened it carefully so he wouldn't compromise any fingerprints on the handle. The refrigerator was full.

Nash and Kitteridge came into the kitchen.

"Nothing," said Nash.

Kitteridge said nothing.

"What?" asked Mac.

"I don't know," said Kitteridge. "There's something creepy about the house. I think it's more than the murders. I don't know."

"Maybe you picked up on something you saw or heard or smelled," said Mac.

"Go with the gut," said Nash.

"This is going to take a while," said Mac. "Keep searching the house. Go with that feeling. Then go ask the neighbors if they saw Shelton. There's an older woman across the street. Her name's Maya

Anderson. She spends a lot of time looking out her window and she knows what Shelton looks like."

"Got it," said Nash, who went back through the door.

Mac took out his cell phone and called Danny.

Danny was at home, sitting in his comfortable chair with the slight tear on the right arm, watching an ancient episode of *The Rockford Files*. His shoes were off and he had a glass of iced tea on the table next to him. The glass rested precariously atop a pile of magazines, mostly old, mostly about forensics. His tremor was still there, but he had the feeling, maybe just a hope, that it was somewhat better. He had taken Sheila Hellyer's advice and another one of the pills. He had also left a note on Mac's desk telling him that he had gone home and why he had done it.

He could tell from Mac's first words that he hadn't yet received the note. Danny hit the mute button on the remote he was holding.

"I'm at the Vorhees house," said Mac. "Shelton was here. He called me."

"You need me there?" asked Danny.

"The knife is here," said Mac. "And we've got to dust everything in the kitchen, contents of the refrigerator, pantry. It's going to take a while."

"I'll be right there," said Danny.

He hung up, sat for a few seconds, looked at James Garner, who seemed exasperated. Danny realized that he had no idea what was happening in the episode. He hit the power button to turn off the TV. He stood, reached for the iced tea, forgetting about the tremor. He knocked the glass over. Tea puddled on the magazines and wooden table and made its way around melting squares of ice.

Danny would clean it up later. He slipped on his shoes, got his kit, which was standing next to the door, and went out into the heat of the day, wondering if Shelton had said anything about what had happened to Jacob Vorhees.

The photographs of the crowds in front of the two temples where the murders had taken place were laid out on the table. There were eighteen of them, eight-by-tens. The photographs were also on a disc, but they wanted to look at them all laid out at the same time.

Flack, Aiden and Stella leaned over them, looking for people who might be in both crowds, searching for possibly familiar faces, scanning each person for a suspicious look, frown, smile.

"That guy, that guy, that woman," said Aiden, pointing at people in the photographs.

One man she had pointed to in the photographs was at least eighty. He had the same sad look in both photographs. Another man was dressed in black, bearded, wearing glasses, definitely Orthodox. He looked somber. None of the others were particularly interesting, but you never knew.

"That's it," said Flack.

"No," said Aiden. "Look at that man."

She pointed to a man in a baseball cap pulled down over his eyes, his hands at his sides. He was wearing dark slacks and a white shirt. He stood between a weeping woman and a black man in a white shirt who craned his neck to get a better view of what was going on. There was a glint of light that suggested the man in the cap was wearing glasses, but it was impossible to clearly see his face or determine his age.

"And here," Aiden said, flipping through the pile of photographs from outside the second crime scene.

She pointed. The man's back was turned, but it was definitely the same man in a baseball cap, same height, shoulders and back straight, military bearing.

"Any other pictures of him?" asked Flack.

"One," said Aiden. "My favorite."

The man was moving away from the camera, looking back over his left shoulder, head down, eyes in the shadow of the brim of his cap, sun glinting from his glasses.

"He's looking at the camera," said Aiden. "And he doesn't want to be recognized."

There was something familiar about him to

Stella. Maybe she was just tired. She knew her allergies were about to kick in and might be fueling her imagination and memory, but she didn't think so.

She looked at the man again and had the eerie sensation that he was looking directly at her.

"Let's blow him up and see what we can see," she said.

Aiden nodded.

6

HAWKES WORKED ON THE BODY OF JOEL BESSER, trying to get Nancy Sinatra singing that damned *Bang Bang* song out of his mind. He had left his iPod at home, forgetting to put it in its plastic case. That had never happened before, and now his punishment was the voice of Nancy Sinatra.

When he removed the two bullets from the skull and held them up with his tweezers, he knew he was dealing with a very small caliber weapon, a small weapon used by someone who knew what he was doing. The shots had been perfectly placed to kill instantly, the same pattern, almost the same location as the shots that had been fired into the head of Asher Glick.

The nails had definitely been driven in post mortem by someone with a strong arm, a left arm according to the angle of the penetration. It didn't take an expert to know that whoever had done this had also killed Asher Glick. Only this time he had not been hurried.

Unlike Glick's case, no member of the Jewish Light of Christ stepped forward to protest an autopsy. So Hawkes was as thorough as he could be.

He always felt like apologizing when he made that first incision. It had to be done. It was not Sheldon Hawkes who was violating the body. Hawkes was giving the dead person on the table a last chance to point a finger at his killer, the one who had fired two bullets into his brain. He made the first incision.

"Bang, bang," came Nancy Sinatra's voice.

They now knew a few things about the man in the baseball cap who had been in the crowds at both murders.

Stella and Aiden hovered over the blowups of the man. The resolution was good, not perfect but good enough to see that the hair at the back of the man's cap was gray. There were also age spots on his visible hand and, in a further blowup, they could make out several hairs growing on the ridge of the man's ear. They both agreed that the man was somewhere between his mid-fifties and sixty-five or even older.

"That shot," Stella said, pointing at one of the photographs. "Pull it up on the screen."

Aiden nodded and started hitting keys. Images

raced by until she found the one Stella had indicated. "What's that on his shirt pocket?"

Aiden started to blow it up. Since the picture of the man was only a small section of a large crowd scene, the image began to lose resolution as Aiden enlarged and focused on what looked like a small gold pin.

"I think we can enhance it a little," said Aiden. "Maybe partial images on other shots, but I think I know what it is."

Stella looked at Aiden, who stared at the photograph.

"I think it's military, a unit pin. My father had one. He never wore it. I'll see what I can find, but there's not much there."

"He stands straight, military," said Stella. "Thick neck."

"He works out," said Aiden.

"Could be our killer," said Stella. "In some of the photographs, he's standing next to people who might remember him."

Aiden knew what she meant. In one of the photographs, the man in the cap was standing next to a man in black, a man with a black beard and hat, a man Stella recognized as being one of the same men she had seen in Asher Glick's congregation.

Stella wiped her nose.

"You too?" asked Aiden, who was feeling the first effects of seasonal allergies in her itchy eyes.

Stella, on the other hand, had a stuffy nose and a slight headache. It wasn't really bad and she knew it wouldn't be, but when she got home, she might have a dose of antihistamine syrup.

She looked again at the photographs of the man in the cap. She had now looked dozens of times, sensing that she had seen him before, but not knowing where. She knew enough to let it alone and hope that it came to her like the name of a movie actor or author you know well but suddenly forget.

"Let's find Flack," Stella said, standing.

Getting a search warrant for Joshua's apartment had been easy after Flack did his research. Judge Obert had signed it when Flack told him the story. The judge was well over seventy and more than ready to retire, but he had hung on through occasional lapses in which he could barely keep himself awake, even on the bench. Regular doses of Modafinil, originally used for narcolepsy, had alleviated the problem, though the judge found himself taking the pill far more often than his doctor had prescribed.

Obert had handed the warrant to Flack, saying with both contempt and resignation, "These people."

Flack didn't want to know who "these people" were. He was sure he would not like the answer.

As he opened the door to Joshua's apartment, Flack went over what he knew. He knew that

Joshua was an alcoholic and had done hard time. His prison medical record, which had come to CSI about an hour ago, showed Joshua had developed lightheadedness and temporary losses of memory. He also had violent episodes and had almost beaten another inmate to death after a disagreement over something Joshua had been unable to remember. Joshua had announced his new name after the attack on the man. No one really gave a shit. Joshua had begun to seek converts, going first to prisoners who had Jewish-sounding names. The effort had almost gotten him killed.

If there were a gun hidden in the apartment, Flack was determined to find it. He knew that there was something different about his relationship to Joshua than to all the suspects he had dealt with before. Part of it was that Joshua was a true believer. Flack didn't trust true believers, especially religious ones—although the political believers and ethnic believers were probably just as dangerous.

True believers were capable of anything because they were sure their cause was just. It was this belief that gave the only meaning to their lives.

Flack knew a lot of true believers in his own family. He had no idea how he had escaped, but he had. From the time he was a boy he had kept his own peace about what he believed. What he believed was between him and God.

*　　*　　*

The man in the cap was back in the deli across from the lab. Actually, he wasn't wearing the cap at the moment. He had exchanged it for one of those tan hats you can crumple and keep in your pocket that always pop back to their original shape, water-proof, ready and with a brim wide enough to pull down over your eyes.

He had also left his glasses at home. The lenses were plain glass. His eyesight was almost perfect. He held the latest copy of *Smithsonian Magazine* in front of him. This would have to be his last visit here, even though he doubted if anyone would re-member him, was even more sure no one would recognize him. He ate slowly, accepting two refills of decaf coffee from the waitress. She looked down at the cap on the chair. He should have left that at home too, but he couldn't bring himself to do it. He was proud of it, probably the last symbol of that part of his life of which he was truly proud. The man smiled at the waitress, who walked to the next table to top off the coffee mug of a heavy-eyed young man in need of a shave and a hairbrush.

It was now three years ago, almost to the day, that the man had placed the jar on the mantel of the fire-place and stepped back to look at it among the pho-tographs. In nearly all of the photographs on the shelf, the people, almost all dead now, were smiling, happy or pretending to be. Some of the people were painfully young. Some were old, holding on to their dignity at least for the duration of that photograph. Some of the young and old were the same people, photos of them taken decades apart.

There had been no religious ceremony, no service. He had wanted none. The grief he felt, the loss, could only be shared with some of the people, now dead, in the photographs. There were people he could talk to, but he had no intention of doing so. He would tolerate no false piety. He wanted no insincere solace nor any promise of an afterlife or eternal memory in which he did not believe. The memory of the person whose ashes lay in that jar would die with him.

He finished his third cup of coffee and looked across the street. She was coming out with that other woman, the pretty, young dark one. As she walked, Stella took a tissue from the pocket of her jacket and wiped her nose.

It wouldn't be long now.

He should have been satisfied, but he had gotten up that morning at dawn as he always did and went to the living room to touch the jar. Something had changed. Something that made him uneasy, but by no means less willing to kill Stella Bonasera.

Mac sat in a straight-backed padded armchair in the living room of the Vorhees house. He had pulled back the curtains to his left to let the sunlight in. He felt the heat on his arm and face.

Danny had finished and gone back to the lab with the knife and a page torn out of Mac's notebook. Danny's tremor was definitely less pronounced, but it was still there and he still had a slightly haunted look in his eyes. Mac had seen that look in the mirror after watching a helicopter attached to his marine unit crash less than fifty yards from where he had been standing. Mac was supposed to be on that copter with eight other marines. He had been pulled off the routine test flight by a marine sergeant who said Mac was wanted in HQ to write a not-very-important report that was due that day. The copter rose about two hundred feet in the air and crashed as Mac and the sergeant who had come for him were about to get into a waiting jeep. Mac and the sergeant ran to the burning wreckage of the mangled copter, which burned brighter as they got closer and suddenly exploded, knocking Mac and the sergeant off their feet.

The next morning Mac had looked in the mirror and seen the haunted look he would see on Danny. The other time he had seen that look in the mirror was just after his wife had died on 9/11.

At the present moment, Mac needed to be alone. To Kyle Shelton it was a deadly serious game. To Mac it was a challenge that could be dealt with by using science and logic.

Art versus science? No, there was definitely an element of art in what Mac and the other CSI detectives did. Art was imagination, creation, an essential element in science, but not a game.

Mac took his notebook from his pocket and opened it to the last page on which he had taken notes.

Approximately 2:45 in the morning, three members of the Vorhees family are murdered with a knife from their kitchen. Why 2:45 a.m.?

The Vorhees' son, Jacob, is missing. Did he hear what was happening? Maybe even open the door to his sister's bedroom and see some or all of what had happened? Did he see Kyle Shelton, his dead family?

ME report shows the dead girl had intercourse, and, judging from the vaginal bruising, the penetration minimal. There were no signs of semen. Was Shelton interrupted by the parents? Was he planning to kill them before he even entered the house? Why did he have a knife from the Vorhees kitchen if he wasn't planning to use it?

Bodies are laid out, women respectfully on the bed, father on the floor in a heap. Likely Shelton's doing but what did it mean?

Garage door is open. Jacob's bicycle is missing. Did Shelton see him, hear him, go after him? Why didn't he catch the boy before he got on the bicycle and rode away?

Neighbor sees Shelton's car drive off heading toward Queens Boulevard. Was he chasing Jacob?

9:25 a.m. the next morning bicycle found along with

Jacob's clothes. One shoe fifty yards from site. Did he lose it running from Shelton? Did Shelton throw it there? Why?

Linden leaf partially chewed by caterpillar and a piece of the insect on the leaf found in boy's bedroom. Leaf did not come from neighborhood. Did it come from site where bicycle and clothes were found? Had it been stuck to Shelton's shoe? Why had he returned to the house later that night? Where is boy or his body?

1:40 p.m. Wednesday Shelton calls the lab from the Vorhees' house to let us know the knife is there. He also makes a remark about having eaten and suggests CSI detective have a snack. Why does Shelton return to the Vorhees house? Why does he leave the knife with his prints? Death wish? Guilt? Part of the game he is playing?

The phone in his pocket vibrated. Mac took it out and opened it.

"That quote," said Danny, "wasn't from Anne Frank. It was from Henry Ward Beecher."

"Thanks," said Mac. "I'm coming in."

It struck Mac as he turned off his phone. This was not a game Shelton was playing to win. He was playing it to lose. The house creaked around him, settled and was still. He had the beginning of an idea. When he had Hawkes' report on the knife and Danny's on the prints, he would be closer to drawing a possible conclusion.

He closed his notebook, put it away and imagined the computer screen with the virtual images of

Shelton and the Vorhees family. He began to move the images around to form a picture they had not considered before.

Aside from the fact that she had pieced together photos of the man in the baseball cap and come up with most of what was written on it, Aiden had found little of interest in what she recovered from the Sirchie vacuum Stella had used on Joel Besser's body. Dust mites, sloughed skin, the usual. There was, however, one thing she had almost missed. It had been tiny and looked like all the other microscopic flotsam you picked up in the city, except this microscopic bit had something about it that looked familiar.

She hunched over the microscope and kept increasing the magnification. She took photographs with the camera mounted on the scope as she moved along.

When she had finished, Aiden carefully placed the glass slide in the slotted box on the table.

No hasty conclusions. She had learned from Mac and Stella that if you have a theory, you test it inside and out and look for evidence.

On the computer screen, Aiden found eight web sites that fit her needs. If she had made the search too broad, she knew she would have come up with thousands of sites.

Before she made her phone call, she called Stella, who answered immediately.

"We've got a name," Aiden said. "It's on his cap. Name is Walke. I think there's a short name or initials before the name, but I can't find an angle to pull them up."

"Walker?" asked Stella. "It might not be his. Could have bought it at a thrift shop."

"I don't think so," said Aiden. "His clothes don't look like thrift shop buys."

"I don't think so either," said Stella. "I'm on my way back."

She flipped her cell phone off.

Aiden went through the eight sites, found exactly what she was looking for and reached for the phone.

There was no problem finding and talking to many of the people in the crowd outside the two scenes of the crucifixion murders. Rabbi Mesmur had helped identify some of them and when Flack and Stella found them they were quite willing to talk, mostly about their theories of who had committed the murders and why.

A woman, Molke Freid, in a long dress, her head covered with a scarf, was at home with her three youngest children five blocks from the synagogue. The other four children were in school. It was obvious that the woman was pregnant and close to delivery.

They sat in the kitchen at a large table, a plate of cookies and a cup of coffee in front of them.

"You want to know who did it?" Molke asked, as if the answer were obvious. "One of those crazies for Jesus."

"Why would they murder one of their own?" Stella asked.

"To create a martyr, to send you looking in the wrong place," the woman said. "They killed Asher Glick. You were investigating them, so they killed one of their own so you would look someplace else."

"Where?" asked Stella.

The cookies were good. Stella was working on her third.

"Or maybe it was anti-Semites," said the woman. "Maybe a group of them, maybe just one. Who knows?"

Flack and Stella nodded. They had, of course, considered this and were checking out groups and individuals who might have committed similar crimes.

"We're looking for a man in a baseball cap," said Flack. "He was standing next to you in the crowd outside the second murder. An older man. Something was written on his cap, possibly Walker."

Molke was shaking her head, her thoughts elsewhere.

"The man in the cap," Stella reminded her.

Molke came back from her reverie, touched her hand to her forehead and looked at them.

"Not Walker," Molke said. "Walke. The words stitched on the man's cap were 'USS *Walke*.' "

Flack jotted that down.

"USS *Walke*," Molke continued. "December 3, 1950. Hit a mine off the east coast of Korea. Twenty-six died, forty were injured. Bad luck ship. In World War II, July 1944, the *Walke* was escorting minesweepers and was attacked by a group of kamikazes. Thirteen members of the crew died, including the captain."

"Are you sure about all this?" asked Flack.

"My uncle had a cap like that," said Molke. "He was proud of his military service and the ship. The *Walke* served combat missions in three wars, World War II, Korea and Vietnam. It was often hit, never sunk. The *Walke* always came back. It was turned into scrap metal in 1976. I asked the man in the cap if he knew my uncle. He said he didn't."

"He give you his name?" asked Flack.

"No," she said. "Just kept looking at the door across the street till you walked out."

The woman was looking at Stella.

"He gave you a long look, then turned and walked away."

When they were back on the street, Flack said, "It doesn't make sense. He's killing Jews because of you?"

"We've seen crazier," she said.

"Watch your back," said Flack. "Hungry?"

"No."

"There's a kosher restaurant over there," said Flack. "Kishke and herring in cream sauce."

It sounded far from appealing, especially the stuffed intestines. Besides, she wanted to get back to the lab and start her search for the man in the cap. She had no intention of focusing only on him. She would check the alibi of every man in the Orthodox congregation and keep up the search for others. Flack could have another shot at Joshua and check to see if the furniture dealer, Arvin Bloom, had an alibi for the time of the second murder.

"Kreplach soup?" Flack tried. "Matzoh ball soup?"

Stella smiled.

"Let's make it fast," she said.

Flack smiled back.

As they crossed the street, Stella didn't tell him that he wouldn't be able to order the two items he wanted. It wasn't kosher to mix dairy products with meat. She had learned that back when she was nineteen and dancing at the Broadway Dance Center. Her friend Ann Ryan, whose real name was Ann Cornridge, had invited her home for dinner not four blocks from where she and Flack were now standing in front of the restaurant. Ann's parents had explained kosher law when Stella had asked if there was butter for her bread.

Stella was sure she remembered seeing this same restaurant fifteen years earlier on the way to Ann's house. New York was a small town if you lived here long enough.

Wearing white latex gloves, Mac carefully laid out the glass fragments taken from the Vorhees' garbage shortly after their initial investigation. The fragments looked like pieces of a three-dimensional jigsaw puzzle, which was how Mac was treating them.

First he had used the spectrometer for signs of blood or fingerprints on any of the fragments. He found none and had given the fragments to Chad Willingham, who took the assignment as a welcome challenge.

Now after a little over two hours Chad had returned with the fragments and a disc that he inserted into the computer, which began to hum, and then an image began to form.

"Scanning electron microscope," Chad said. "You can enlarge any microscopic surface or any part of a surface."

Mac nodded, looking at the screen covered not in enlarged fragments but tiny images that filled the page.

"Can enlarge any piece," Chad said with pride, moving the mouse to a random image and clicking.

The tiny fragment now filled the screen. Chad moved the three-dimensional image around so that Mac could see all sides.

"Neat, huh?" asked Chad.

Mac nodded.

"You ain't seen nothing yet," said Chad, who pressed a series of keys. The tiny fragments on the screen moved rapidly, came together. Chad enlarged the image.

Now Mac knew what had bruised the arm and dented the bone of Howard Vorhees.

"Print three of them," said Mac.

"Print three of them," Chad sang.

The printer next to the computer hummed to life and three full-color eight-by-ten pictures of the object emerged.

Mac gathered them, put them in an envelope. He had people to show the pictures to.

"OK if I put the real fragments together?" asked Chad.

"Maybe when the case is closed," said Mac.

Chad nodded in understanding and said, "Can I ask you a question?"

"Yes," said Mac.

"You ever dream about dying horses?"

Mac was used to Chad's non sequiturs, but this one was different.

"Yes," said Mac.

"So do I," said Chad. "I wonder what it means."

It wasn't a question Mac had ever really asked himself and he didn't intend to do so now, although the dream image of the collapsing horse pulling a fire truck flashed through his head.

7

MAC SAT AT THE KITCHEN TABLE, red and white check-
ered cloth on top of it, plus two cups of coffee, one
for him and one for Maya Anderson. He had placed
the envelope on the table in front of her.

"Tell me again what you saw this morning."

"Nothing," she said. "I was sitting by the window, looking out, listening to music on my stereo.
Show tunes. You like show tunes?"

"Some," said Mac patiently.

"My favorite is still *Oklahoma*," she said. "Second
musical my mother took me to. First was
Brigadoon."

"This morning?" Mac said gently.

"I'm just playing with you," the woman said,
leaning forward as if it were a secret. "You get away
with a lot when you get old."

Mac nodded.

"You knew I was playing, right?" she asked.

"Yes," said Mac. "This morning," he prodded.

"Nothing," she said. "No unfamiliar cars on the street. Nobody but you and the police going in the house or coming out."

"You didn't see Kyle Shelton go into the Vorhees' house?"

"Nor come out," she added. "He could have come through the back, through the kitchen, or he could have gone in there late at night when I got a few hours of sleep. But I did see him the night he killed everybody. I'd swear it on a Bible."

"You might have to do just that. Doors of the Vorhees house were locked," said Mac. "So were the windows."

"Like Yul Brynner said in *The King and I*," said Maya, "it's a puzzlement. Maybe he had a key. Maybe someone let him in. No, there's no one in there."

Mac unclasped the envelope on the table, opened it and removed the printout of a colorful Asian flowered vase.

"You recognize this?" he asked.

"No," she said. "Should I?"

"We think it was in the Vorhees house."

"Search me," Maya said with a shrug. "I could count the number of times I've been in there on the fingers of my late brother Arthur's right hand. He only had two fingers and a thumb."

"You'll keep watching?" asked Mac.

"Would even if you didn't ask," she said.

"Thank you," he said, carefully putting the picture of the vase back in the envelope and getting up.

Outside Mac opened his notebook, found the number he needed and punched it in and waited.

Maybelle Rose said, "Yes?"

Mac described the vase in the photo he held up in front of him.

"One black little flower right near the top?"

"Yes," said Mac.

"That was Becky's. Mr. Vorhees gave it to her after a business trip to Tokyo last year."

"Where was it kept in the house?" he asked.

"Becky's bedroom on the dresser," said Maybelle. "You find Jacob?"

"Not yet," said Mac, but he thought it would be soon.

"I pray he's alive," said Maybelle.

Mac thought the boy was alive. He was close to knowing it with some certainty, but he needed the help of a friend.

Professor of botany Leo Dobrint looked up at Aiden and said, "Do you mind sitting down?"

They were in Dobrint's small laboratory/office at Columbia University. The room was hot and had a bitter, acidic smell. Given a choice between that smell and the blood and body odors of some of the dead she routinely encountered, a decision would be hard.

Dobrint, in his sixties, thin, wearing jeans and a heavy wool shirt in apparent defiance of the weather, was sitting in front of a microscope looking at what Aiden had brought him. Dobrint's hair was salt-and-pepper, mostly salt, and he could definitely have used a haircut.

He was also definitely irritable. She sat in the chair he pointed to a few feet away and went back to the microscope.

After five minutes or so of adjusting, mumbling to himself, he looked up at her and said, "That is the smallest specimen I've ever been asked or chosen to look at."

Aiden waited.

"Yes," he said. "It's bloodwood. It's been treated and preserved. It comes, most likely, from a piece of furniture or from a bloodwood floor."

"Could you match it to a specific piece of furniture?" Aiden asked.

"Bloodwood is bloodwood," he said with slight irritation.

"If you had the piece of furniture," she said, "could you match it to this specimen?"

"Like a jigsaw puzzle," he said. "Highly unlikely. It's too small."

"Unlikely but not impossible," said Aiden.

"That's right," he said.

"Are you willing to give it a try?" she asked.

"I'm very—" he began, but Aiden interrupted.

"Two men were shot and crucified in the last three days. If you can match these pieces . . ."

"I can try," he said with a sigh.

"You'll be paid as an expert consultant."

"Of course," he said. "My fee will depend on how long it takes and how much trouble I run into."

"Bill us," she said flatly.

Danny wanted to stay away from the lab but he kept getting ideas, "what if?" ideas. There was a twelve-year-old boy missing. His family had been murdered. An image of the slaughter scene flashed in his mind. He willed it to go away. Mercifully, it did.

"You all right?" Chad Willingham asked, turning from the pile of clothes spread out on the table in front of him.

He had run the boy's clothing that had been found in the woods through more tests. They had just come out of the gas chromatograph.

"Fine," said Danny.

"Suit yourself," said the lab tech in the white coat. "I believe in minding my own business." He paused and added, "And everyone else's."

"Lights," he said, putting on a pair of wrap-around amber plastic glasses. He handed another pair to Danny.

Danny moved to the wall and turned off the lights. Chad moved back to the table with Danny behind him and switched on a ceiling-mounted red light.

"I've come to two conclusions," said Chad seriously. "And I'm about to make a third."

"What are they?" asked Danny.

Chad grinned and carefully moved around the clothing, examining the items, smelling them. At one point he put a finger in his mouth to moisten it, touched the pullover shirt and the underwear and smelled his finger.

"Three conclusions," Danny reminded him.

"Yes," said Chad, raising his eyebrows and continuing a careful examination of the underwear, T-shirt, jeans, socks and shoes.

"First," said Chad. "The Who were definitely the best. Beatles, Grateful Dead, Stones, great, but The Who, immortal. I have an uncle who almost went deaf at one of their concerts."

"Second conclusion?" asked Danny, trying not to show signs of impatience.

"You've got a tremor in your right hand," Chad said, leaning over the spread-out clothing. "Come take a look."

Danny moved to the table.

"What was I . . . ," said Chad. "Tremor."

"You noticed," said Danny with a touch of irritation.

"Cop's syndrome number four," said Chad.

"It has a name and number?" said Danny.

"I gave it one," said Chad. "Job stress. I've noticed it more lately, started with 9/11. It goes away or it doesn't. You see Sheila Hellyer?"

"I saw her," Danny said. "What did you want me to look at here?"

Danny was standing at Chad's side in front of the table.

"Pants, underwear, socks, shirt," Chad said, pointing at each item. "Latent signs of grass, insect fecal matter, dirt, residue from a joint smoked at least four or five days before you found the evidence. But that's not what's interesting."

He pointed to the shirt on the table and said, "What do you see?"

"Bloodstains," said Danny.

"Anything else?"

"No," said Danny.

"You got it," said Chad. "I owe you a Thai dinner when I get my next upgrade. Make it the one after that. These clothes only show signs of dirt where they were dropped."

"So?" asked Danny, wanting to take off the glasses, get out of the room.

"So," said Chad. "There should have been something, not much, but something—dirt, leaves, grass, weeds—on the clothes other than where they lay on the ground."

"I still don't—" Danny began.

"The shirt shows traces from those woods on the front," said Chad. "The pants show traces only on the back. The underwear shows traces only on the front, and the shoes are the oddest of all. One has scene traces on the bottom. The other shoe shows it on the side."

Danny cursed himself silently and went to the computer, where he pulled up photos of where they had found Jacob Vorhees' bicycle and clothing. He should have thought of this before.

"What?" asked Chad over his shoulder.

Danny went slowly through all twenty-three photographs and then sat back. If Kyle Shelton had undressed the boy or forced him to take his clothes off, why were they all over the scene?

"They were thrown around to make it look random," said Danny. "Maybe Jacob Vorhees was never in the woods."

"Way I see it too," said Chad, "but wait, there's more. You know what that is?"

Chad was pointing at a small, black-plastic-covered box at the edge of the table.

"STU-100, scent transfer unit," said Danny.

"Right, almost forgot," said Chad, hitting his forehead with an open palm. "You're a crime scene investigator."

Inside the portable forensic vacuum was a slot for five-by-nine-inch sterile gauze pads. The airflow system provided a safe method for collecting human scents from small objects, clothing, bodies, windowsills. Human scent particles, gaseous or airborne, could be moved to the pad using the vacuum in much the same way as smell. Breathing creates a vacuum that draws odors into nasal passages, where the smell kicks in.

"Human scent," said Chad, "has historically been defined as a biological component of decomposing dead skin cells, the skin raft theory."

"I know," said Danny with exaggerated patience.

"Current research suggests human body odor is much more complex," said Chad. "Like Latin."

"Latin?"

"Well, it was complex for me," said Chad.

"The STU," Danny reminded him.

"Right," said Chad. "Scents collected from expended cartridge casings in drive-by shooting cases have been used to track down the shooter. Collected the scent of Jacob Vorhees from the shoes and the scent of Kyle Shelton from the samples of his clothing you brought from his apartment. No trace of the boy's scent on the clothes. But," said Chad, holding up a finger, "they had been touched. The only human scent on the shorts, shirt and jeans was Kyle Shelton's."

"Shelton wore the boy's clothes?" asked Danny.

"How could he . . . ," Chad began. "You're kidding me."

"I'm kidding you," said Danny. "Shelton handled the boy's clothes."

"A conundrum that echoes through the history of life's vagaries," said Chad.

Danny nodded. Chad wanted to say more but saw that he did not have an attentive audience.

"I'll run your samples through the gas chromatograph," said Chad.

Danny nodded and headed for the door as Chad said, "You like Barenaked Ladies?"

"Who doesn't?" said Danny.

"Sexist," said Chad.

"I'll live with it," said Danny.

Chad noticed that Danny's hand was no longer trembling. Danny wouldn't notice for another ten minutes, after he had called Mac to tell him about the clean clothes and the scent of Shelton but not the boy on them.

"Fits," said Mac.

Danny wasn't sure how, not until Mac explained.

Stella entered her apartment. It was still relatively early in the day, but she knew she needed at least a few hours' sleep. It wasn't just her allergies. She had been working long days and knew that if she got too tired she might well miss something. It had happened to her before. Mac had on more than one occasion ordered her to get some rest. She had learned less from her trust in his judgment than from her experience when she didn't get at least a minimum of sleep.

She kicked off her shoes and left them by the door. Her plan was to drink some bottled water, eat a banana yogurt and a slice of toast, and get out of her clothes.

She hadn't finished locking her door when she sensed that something was different. It wasn't ESP. Stella knew that even a minimal human or animal scent would be registered by the brain. So too with the flow of air if furniture had been moved. Or a slight move of an object—furniture, a vase of flowers, one of the paintings on her walls. She considered taking her gun out of her holster. What was the line from that old *Night Stalker* episode? "If you don't look up, maybe it's not there." Stella turned into the room and looked up.

The list of people who might be seeking revenge for having been caught by her over the years was long. Then again, it could be a burglar or even the building superintendent, who had been told not to enter her apartment without her permission.

Her paintings, paintings she loved and had picked up over the years in Europe, seemed to be in place. They were not without value, but they probably were not worth more than a few thousand each. She had never had them appraised. They were not an investment.

She moved cautiously to her kitchen, everything in place, cabinet doors closed. Nothing in the refrigerator—not that there was much there—seemed to have been touched. The clothes in her bedroom closet and her drawers did not seem to have been moved and her bed was well and tightly made as she had learned to do in the orphanage. Then she moved to the bathroom. She thought there was a trace of a scuff mark on the tile floor but she couldn't be sure. She got her kit and carefully took a sample of the material from the scuff mark.

Paranoia, she decided when she was sure she was the only one in the apartment. I'm tired, paranoid and allergic to much that exists in the world. She sneezed and moved to the medicine cabinet in the small bathroom. She definitely needed some antihistamine. Stella opened the cabinet door, saw what she was looking for and reached for the bottle.

Flack stood in front of the counter of the electronics store and listened patiently to the man who was speaking with a heavy Indian accent. The man was short, dark, thick head of hair, bad skin and about forty. He was also perspiring. His name was Al Chandrasekhar.

"I'm a second cousin of the famous physicist," Chandrasekhar said proudly.

Flack nodded.

The small shop was crowded with glassed-in cell phones, walkie-talkies, tiny radios, tape recorders that could fit in a side pocket or purse, electronic toys, compact computers and printers, cameras and clocks. There were two potential customers at the rear of the shop, a boy and girl in their twenties, casually dressed.

Flack counted five video cameras around the shop. None were hidden. Chandrasekhar wanted potential thieves to know they were being watched.

"You have some information about who killed those two men?" asked Flack.

"I'm sorry I called 911," the man said. "I know it wasn't an emergency, or perhaps it was. It is really for you to decide."

Flack waited.

"I have two video cameras mounted outside my store," the man said, looking toward the open front door through which warm air flowed, was spun by two ceiling fans, and was replaced by another stealthy wave of heat. "One is mounted so that it picks up the front of that store where the Jewish Jesus man was murdered."

"Let's take a look," said Flack.

Chandrasekhar reached under the counter and pulled out a videotape. He put the tape in a compact player on a shelf behind the counter. He pressed a button and the image appeared.

"You see there?" the man said with excitement, pointing to a figure on the screen.

It was Stella and Flack. They came out of the storefront talking, heading up the street to their left. Flack could see steam rising from the sidewalk. The crowd was gone. When the body went, so did the gathering.

"Now," said Chandrasekhar, "there."

He pointed to someone who came out of a doorway, turned to his left and walked slowly about thirty yards behind Flack and Stella.

"Here," said Chandrasekhar. "You turn your head and the man pauses to look in a store window. In that store is sold Jewish books. I'm saying to myself, this man does not look Jewish. This man is following you."

For an instant, as he paused by the bookstore window, the man looked back, facing the camera. From the poor quality of the tape, Flack wasn't sure how much they would be able to blow up the image, but there were two things Flack could make out. The first was that the man had salt-and-pepper gray hair. The second was that a baseball cap was protruding from the man's left rear pocket. It wouldn't be hard to confirm that this was the same man who had appeared in the crowd at both murder sites.

But, thought Flack, why is he following us?

"That's almost an hour after the murder," said

Flack, concentrating again on the tape, which showed the date and time in the lower left-hand corner.

"Killer returns to scene," said Chandrasekhar with a slow nod of his head meant to show wisdom.

"Let's go back on the tape," said Flack.

The two customers in the back were heading toward the front door. They glanced at Flack. He knew they had pegged him as a cop, which was fine with him.

The man behind the counter rewound and Flack watched at fast speed. People passed on the street and entered and left the storefront synagogue. Everyone who entered and left was a member of the congregation. No one entered or left from the moment the congregants went off for lunch and meditation till they returned an hour later.

No surprise there. Stella had agreed that the killer came through the back door. Something tugged at Flack's memory.

"Go back to the time just before they went to lunch," he said.

"Roger that," said the man, hitting the rewind button.

Flack watched people move slowly down the street in both directions. Then he saw the image that had tugged his memory. From the angle of the camera, Flack could only see the back of the big man carrying a briefcase, but what he saw was familiar. The man didn't stop at the synagogue but walked on and entered a doorway at his right.

"What's in that shop?" asked Flack, pointing to the image.

Chandrasekhar took a pair of rimless glasses from a case in his pocket and looked at the frozen image on the screen.

"The newspaper and sundries shop of Mr. Pyon," he said. "He's from Korea. Don't know him well."

"Does he have video cameras?" asked Flack.

"It would be unwise not to," said the man knowingly.

"Can I take the tape?" Flack asked.

Chandrasekhar removed the tape from the machine and handed it to Flack, who pocketed it and headed for the door.

8

THE PHONE RANG.

Stella, who had fallen asleep in her living room while looking up at her paintings, answered, "Detective Bonasera."

"George Harbaugh, FBI," the man said. "Just got your crime scene photographs and preliminary report on the death of the two Jewish men. Good work."

"Thanks," said Stella, trying to wake up.

"I think you may be looking for a serial killer we've been after for three years," Harbaugh said. "I've been authorized to give you a copy of our report. Our profilers think he's going to kill again soon."

Harbaugh was bypassing the chain of command by going to Stella. This was not the first time it had happened.

She said, "Give me a little time and I'll meet you at—"

"I'd prefer to keep the FBI out of this for now," Harbaugh said. "I can be at your apartment later tonight."

She did not ask him how he knew where she lived. An FBI agent would have no trouble finding her.

"I hand you the report and you can ask some questions," he said. "No guarantee I'll answer them."

"You drink tea?" she asked.

"Hate the stuff," he said.

"Coffee?"

"Coke, if you've got it," he said.

"Fine," she said.

He hung up. So did Stella. She got up and moved toward the bedroom, phone in hand. She had a lot to do in the next hour.

In the darkness, Jacob Vorhees uncrossed his aching legs and looked at the green glow of the battery-operated clock on the floor in front of him. He had a pillow and two blankets, one to lie on and one to cover himself with. In addition to the clock, there was a small blue-and-white plastic box inside of which were an ice pack, eight peanut-butter-and-black-currant-jelly sandwiches and ten plastic twelve-ounce bottles of Coke. There was also a white plastic bucket which, in an emergency, he could use as a toilet. A nearly full roll of toilet paper sat next to it. Finally, there was his MP3 player, which he listened to for long, blackened hours.

Behind him, a dozen or more feet away, something scurried. He knew it was rats, more than one. So far they hadn't bothered him, although once, during the night while he slept, he was awakened by a single rat running past him.

He had bolted up, immediately awake and breathing hard, seeing Becky and his mother bleeding, dying.

I'm twelve years old, he told himself. Things like this shouldn't happen to a kid. Then he remembered the television images of the dying people of Africa, the near skeletons that once were children and were now large-headed, wide-eyed, open-mouthed, blank-staring soon-to-be corpses. One of the sandwiches in the cooler near him might be able to save a child in Niger, but Jacob knew this was not a realistic possibility. Jacob lived in a hell no child should have to endure, but there were others whose hell was even deeper and darker than Jacob's. He kept telling himself this, rocking back and forth, arms wrapped around himself.

Something, someone moved, not a rat in the tunnel, but someone on the other side of the wall. The wooden floors of the room creaked with almost every footstep.

Kyle's coming back, Jacob thought, taking the pillow in his arms, not for protection but for comfort.

Then Jacob heard another sound on the other side of the wall, a sound he couldn't make out, like . . . a dog sniffing.

Why would Kyle bring a dog here?

The news shop owner wanted to cooperate. He longed to cooperate. He sweated to cooperate with Flack.

The shop was small. So was the Korean man behind the counter, who knew he was sweating but was afraid to wipe his neck and brow, afraid the determined-looking policeman might think him guilty of something. In North Korea, Sak Pyon had lost most of his family by the 1980s. His mother, his brother, his oldest son, all of whom committed the crime of insufficient enthusiasm for Communism, at least in the minds of the five men in loose brown uniforms who came to his home just before sunrise on a day almost as hot as this one.

The five men, all barely men at all, had let Pyon, his wife and his daughter live to tend the rice field. But Pyon and what remained of his family knew they would be back, would almost certainly kill them. Pyon, his wife and his daughter had trekked through boggy fields of sickly rice and forests of skeleton trees and skirted villages, expecting to be shot from behind as traitors. After six weeks, moving only at night, they had made it to the forty-eighth parallel, crawled past the North Korean guards and almost been shot by the South Korean guards as they crossed the border.

It took four years working at the American embassy to finally be granted political asylum in the United States.

"Videotape," said Flack, pointing up at a camera aimed at them and waking Pyon from his reverie.

"They don't work," said Pyon. "They just have a battery that powers the green light you see. Too much money to get real ones. Don't need them."

He had only a slight accent.

"And if you get robbed or shot?"

"I become less able to provide for my family," said Pyon. "And if I'm shot, I have insurance if I am not killed."

Pyon glanced at his watch. It was one of his two golf days. His wife would be in soon to relieve him so he could take the train to Queens and go to the golf course, where his clubs sat in a locker he rented. Golf was his meditation, an exercise in skill and precision. It was about losing oneself in the stroke and, at the end, finding a great satisfaction if a stroke or two could be cut from the last outing's score.

"What about catching the robbers?" asked Flack with resignation.

"They will no longer have my merchandise or

money," Pyon said, hoping the sweat wasn't streaming down his face as he imagined it was.

"What about them paying for shooting you?"

"It does me and my family no good," said Pyon. "And I have insurance. I abandoned vengeance when I was in Korea."

"Okay," said Flack with a sigh. "Did you recognize the man?"

"Never saw him before," said Pyon.

Flack neither believed nor disbelieved him. He had dealt with Asian refugees before. They were very good at lying. They had been taught how to do it in the hells of places like North Korea and Laos.

"So you couldn't identify him?" asked Flack.

"Yes."

"Yes you could or yes you couldn't?" Flack said, calling on his reserves of patience.

Flack hadn't had much sleep in the last twenty-four hours. To be precise, he had slept for approximately two hours and forty-eight minutes.

"Yes, I could," said Pyon, no longer able to maintain control.

He pulled a large, crumpled white handkerchief from his pocket and wiped his face and neck. Flack took his own already moist handkerchief out and did the same.

"It's almost a hundred and four degrees out there," said Flack, pocketing his handkerchief.

Pyon nodded.

"If you like," said Pyon. "I could draw a picture of the man. I've been taking art courses."

Flack smiled and said, "I'd like you to draw a picture of the man."

"Now?" asked Pyon.

Pyon was trying hard to be cooperative, or at least appear to be.

"Now would be perfect," said Flack. "You want to lock up for a while? I'll take you someplace air-conditioned for a sandwich and coffee."

"Scrambled eggs and Dr Pepper," said Pyon. "Ginsberg's is just around the corner."

Aiden had been right.

"Yes," said Jane Parsons, looking at the packet Aiden had handed her. "Trees have DNA. It's been used a few times as forensic evidence. Landmark case by a professor at Purdue University. It held up in court."

Aiden smiled.

"You think this might be from a piece of furniture?" asked Jane.

"A piece of furniture made out of bloodwood," said Aiden.

"I'll check the DNA. Tannic acid levels should be precisely the same in both specimens regardless of the type of tree we're talking about. The same is true of arsenic levels."

"Arsenic is in trees?" asked Aiden.

"Before it became illegal to do so," said Jane, "arsenic was liberally sprayed on trees and furniture to protect them. Magnesium levels should also be the same in both sources. It's going to take a little time."

"How much time?" asked Aiden.

"This is a very small sample. Three days, maybe only two," said Jane. "I'll need a sample of whatever you want me to compare it with as soon as possible."

"I'll get it," Aiden said. "Then you'll have to work fast. In three days, he may kill again."

"I'll need approval from Mac to move this to the top," said Jane.

"I'll get that too," Aiden said.

She made the call to Mac. It was after dark, but she was sure he wouldn't mind. He didn't. He gave her permission to move to the top of the testing chain. She handed the phone to Jane who said, "Yes?"

That was all she said. The call took no more than a few seconds.

"There was something wrong with the connection," Jane said with a sigh as Aiden put her phone away.

"He was whispering," Aiden said.

The next question that either could have asked of the other was 'Why?' but neither did.

Aiden strode to the door and out. It was getting late but she knew Arvin Bloom and his wife lived above his shop and she was reasonably certain they went out very little, if at all. The shambling pale Bloom had a languid, sedentary look.

Aiden knew there were some holes in her theory. First, the killer was left-handed. Bloom was right-handed. Second, if Bloom had an alibi for the murder of Joel Besser, she had a major problem. Third, both killings had looked like the work of a professional—two small-pattern shots to the back of the head. A pro who was also some kind of religious nut, or a professional pretending to be. They had run a background check on Arvin Bloom. He seemed a very unlikely hit man.

When she ran his prints they matched to a job application that told her Arvin Bloom was fifty-three years old, a native of Tacoma, Washington, who had earned an undergraduate degree in botany at the University of Washington. No military record. No criminal record, not even a moving vehicle violation, at least none they could find. He had a wife, no siblings, no cousins, and his parents were dead, father from a heart attack, mother from lung cancer. Arvin Bloom had gone through six jobs in the past twenty years, making his way across the country, working as a carpenter, home builder, cabinet maker, and finally an owner of a furniture restoration shop in Manhattan. He had a weapons permit, which was the reason Aiden had found his fingerprints. Aiden had seen the gun, a .45 mm handgun that looked and smelled as if it had never been fired. Most shop owners in Manhattan had gun permits. The gun that had been used to kill Glick and Besser was a .33 mm.

There were other holes in the theory and she wasn't giving up on Joshua, the man in the USS *Walke* cap or some third person they hadn't even considered yet.

The cell phone she had placed in the cup holder by the steering wheel rang.

"Bloodwood," Jane said, and hung up.

Before she could put the phone back in the cup holder it rang again.

"Got a drawing of the guy on the tape who went through the magazine shop," said Flack. "Pyon, the guy who owns the place, is good enough to be a police sketch artist."

"Is it Arvin Bloom?" asked Aiden.

Flack reached into a folder under his arm, opened it and pulled out the drawing. It didn't look like Bloom. The man in the drawing was gaunt, receding hairline, about thirty, probably Hispanic, clean shaven.

"Could be any of a million people in this city," he said. "And he's not on our radar in this case. At least he wasn't till now."

"Bloom?" asked Flack.

"I'm not giving up on him. I'm on my way over to his place now," she said.

"Then so am I," said Flack. "You call Stella?"

"I'll do it now," said Aiden. "We'll wait for her to meet us."

Danny sat back in his chair in the dark, a sandwich in one hand, the remote in the other. He had forgotten what kind of sandwich he was eating. He adjusted his glasses, eyes on the glowing screen. Baseball game. The Mets. He didn't know the score or what inning it was. The announcer said, "It's more than hot out there today. The Mets' white uniforms have turned gray from the sweat."

Danny was wearing a pair of boxer shots an ex-girlfriend had given him. The shorts were black with penguins marching all over. Danny looked down at his New York Mets T-shirt and thought about his grandfather, the one with the tremor diagnosed as Parkinson's. His grandfather had been a cop. His father had been a cop. The Messer men and a few of the women had been NYPD going back for generations.

Danny was tired, needed a shave, wondered if he could still throw a decent slider and changeup. He had been a genuine prospect ten years ago. He was encouraged by three major league teams. Then his arm went and along with it, after surgery, his fastball. He had been consistently clocked at ninety miles an hour, but now he knew he would be lucky to throw at eighty, which, for most major league pitchers, was just a changeup.

He remembered the can of Sprite on the table, put down the remote and took a sip. The tremor was back, almost undetectable.

Then, with no warning, Danny was having an anxiety attack. He had had three attacks in his life. He put his head between his legs and took long, slow breaths until he was back under control. He stayed with his head bowed for a few minutes more, then stood suddenly.

He wanted, needed to find something to do, but he knew he couldn't get in bed, couldn't sleep, couldn't listen to music, couldn't watch the game. He considered getting dressed and finding a twenty-four-hour restaurant where he could sit with other customers, or at least a waiter, and nurse a decaf coffee and a donut.

He moved to the table in the corner on which his computer sat. There was more room in the bedroom, but Mac had once suggested that one shouldn't work in the same room in which one slept.

Danny sat, touched the mouse; the monitor gave off three tones that were meant to be calming, and the screen lit up.

He browsed for more than an hour, following a thread about the decision to drop the atomic bombs on Japan, then he switched to a search for Kyle Shelton. There were dozens of Google hits, none that matched their suspect. He narrowed the search to "Kyle Shelton, philosophy."

He still got a long list of sites, but the first one brought Danny awake. He cleaned his glasses on his Mets shirt and found out some things that had not turned up in the routine bio check.

Kyle Shelton had a web site. At the top of the home page were three black-and-white photographs of a pair of hands. In the photograph on the left, the hands were open palms facing the camera. In the center photograph, the hands were folded in what appeared to be prayer. And in the last photograph, the hands were tightly clenched, knuckles white. Anger?

There was a comment in script just below the photographs. It read:

Imagine a vast valley full of rocks, boulders, as far as the eye can see in any direction. Now, imagine a butterfly the size of a baby's hand with wings so thin you can see through them. The butterfly lands on one boulder the size of a Volkswagen and begins fluttering its wings against the boulder, slowly, imperceptibly, wearing down the boulder. When the boulder is finally gone after more than ten times as long as life has existed on earth, the butterfly moves on to the next boulder, which is even larger than the first. When all the boulders and rocks have been worn to dust by the fluttering wings, then, and only then, will eternity have begun.

Beneath the words was typed in regular text, "Suggested by a passage in Ugo Betti's *Crime on Goat Island.*"

Danny reread the paraphrased quotation and felt somewhat calmed by it. Kyle Shelton was also a blogger. Danny clicked on the image for the blog site. A check of past entries showed that the site was kept up to date, a new entry at least once a week. There were no more than a few dozen responses to Shelton's stream-of-consciousness meandering. Danny read Shelton's entries, forgetting his anxiety. Some of the entries were about philosophers, dead philosophers with whom Shelton agreed or disagreed. There were quotations from philosophers in every entry.

The entries were full of contradictions. Shelton did not believe in the goodness of man, but in the near sainthood of many individuals. He said he had learned that in Iraq. He did not believe in any religion, but he cited evidence of the power of prayer. The entries were all calm, not frenetic, not someone trying to convince his reader, but someone who felt the need to send his thoughts to the wind.

There was only one subject about which Kyle Shelton raged: child abuse. Shelton did not consider human life sacred. There were many, mostly those who abused children, who Kyle said "should simply, painlessly, be executed, burned and their remains dumped into the nearest toilet."

Danny kept reading, hand steady, focused.

William Wosak, SJ, thirty-eight, was a scholar-priest with a Ph.D. from Fordham. Wosak had written three books. His area of interest was correcting false conceptions and misreadings from holy scripture. Father Wosak, lean and graying, wore an almost constant bemused smile.

He was certain that most lay Catholics did not read the Gospels, and certainly not the writings of the saints, with an interest in learning. They read, those that did, to find in what they read and what they heard in church on Sundays confirmation of what they had learned from their parents and misinformed nuns and priests who taught them as children.

Catholicism was not in need of reform. It was the pervasive ignorance of Catholics about their religion that was in need of attention. Father Wosak also hoped that his writing would be read by the clergy of other religions. He wanted other Christians, Jews, Muslims, Hindus and even atheists to understand, to be informed by his scholarship, not to get them to embrace Catholicism but to get them to understand what the religion really means. He expected very little success. It was enough that God had set him to his task and given him the intellect to undertake it.

William Wosak's parents were immigrants from Poland. Both were dead. Father Wosak had no siblings, only an aunt and uncle who had never left a small town outside of Warsaw.

He had volunteered, both as part of his research

and to strengthen his faith, to fill in for Father Cabrera at St. Martine's in Brooklyn for a year. He was in his fifth month at the church and it had turned out to be even more than he had hoped.

Most of the congregation spoke Spanish. No problem for Father Wosak, who spoke fluent Spanish, Italian, Polish, German, Hebrew and rather rusty Latin. He conducted mass and services in Spanish.

In his second week at St. Martine's, Father Wosak had made an appointment with Rabbi Benzion Mesmur, whose synagogue was six blocks from St. Martine's. The thirty-eight-year-old priest had introduced himself with respect for the eighty-one-year-old rabbi. Rabbi Mesmur had planned to make the meeting brief and remain in the small lobby of the synagogue.

Father Wosak had spoken in Hebrew and Rabbi Mesmur responded in kind. It struck him that no one in his congregation spoke better conversational Hebrew than this priest. The smiling priest seemed to have no accent, while Rabbi Mesmur was well aware of the tinge of Crown Heights that clung to his Hebrew and would always be there.

Within three minutes, the two men had spoken of the priest's interest. In his three file drawers, the rabbi knew he had at least forty sermons and as many as fifteen speeches on the misreading of the Scriptures and the Talmud.

It was clear that the priest's interest in the Talmud and its teachings came close to that of the old rabbi.

They moved to the rabbi's office and spoke for two hours. The priest returned on a weekly basis. Rabbi Mesmur looked forward to the meetings and their arguments over interpretation of holy writings. They never met at St. Martine's. Father Wosak never suggested it. He knew the rabbi would have to refuse. The moment would be awkward.

They had not had their usual meeting this week, but today Father Wosak felt that with two days passing, he could stop by briefly and give his condolences.

Rabbi Mesmur looked frail, his age increased by tragedy.

Rabbi Mesmur had insisted that the priest join him in his office. For reasons neither man could explain, they spoke in English.

"My congregation prayed for you and your loss," said Father Wosak. "I hope that was acceptable."

Rabbi Mesmur lifted a hand from the arm of his chair and said with almost a smile, "It can't hurt. And the misguided young dead boy who believed in Joshua's rantings?"

"We prayed for him too," said Father Wosak.

In the past, both men had spoken of the Jews for Jesus and Joshua. Both men had rejected the passionate overtures of Joshua and his followers to accept them. Rabbi Mesmur had refused to engage in discussion with Joshua, but Father Wosak had gladly allowed himself to be engaged in discussion with the man. It wasn't a matter of Joshua and his people trying to convert the Catholic priest as it was with Rabbi Mesmur's congregation. The Catholics already accepted Yeshua as their savior. But, like Rabbi Mesmur, Father Wosak did not believe one could be a Jew and a Christian at the same time.

Father Wosak had realized early in the conversation with Joshua that the man was only superficially knowledgeable about both Judaism and Christianity. But it was not just the man's ignorance that caused the priest to stop engaging in any further confrontations or discussions with Joshua. Fanaticism had been in the eyes of Joshua, a burning fanaticism. Joshua had wide-open eyes that couldn't stay focused for more than a few seconds.

With great reluctance, but with an understanding that he must do it, when Father Wosak left the synagogue he would walk the two blocks to the Jewish Light of Christ and express his condolences.

Half a block away, plastic cup of tepid coffee in one hand and a copy of the *Post* in front of his face, the man leaned against a wall next to a small kosher Chinese restaurant. His eyes seemed focused on the stories of mayhem, corruption and tragedy. He

turned a page and took a sip of coffee without looking up. He had checked the thermometer in a re-
sale shop window on the way here. The
temperature was one hundred and one. The sky
was clear, but the air moist. It had been the same
for the past two weeks. People moved slowly, people who had to be outdoors or had a high tolerance
for heat and humidity. Perspiration formed a
beaded rain forest around his hairy chest.

The man he was waiting for came out of the
building he was watching on the other side of the
street and started down the sidewalk.

The man across the street would be the next to
be symbolically crucified.

It would have to be done soon. One more death
and it would be finished. He pushed away from the
wall, dropped the coffee cup in a trash basket,
tucked the newspaper under his arm and felt the
weight of the bolts in one pocket and the heft of
the hammer in the other.

The priest walked briskly. On the opposite side of
the street, the man followed.

9

"You know where Jacob is, don't you?" asked Kyle Shelton, who spoke slowly, drained.

Mac sat in the chair in the Vorhees living room, a cell phone to his ear. His temporary partner sat silently as darkness fell.

"Yes," said Mac.

"Then I'm going to disappear," said Shelton.

"Not possible," said Mac.

"Then you'll catch me," he said. "I'll tell you then what I tell you now. I killed them, Becky, her mom and her father. My prints are on the knife."

Mac was silent.

"You there, Taylor?" Shelton asked.

"I'm here."

"You think I'm a monster, Taylor?"

There was a touch of pleading in his voice.

" 'He who fights with monsters should look to it

that he himself does not become a monster,' " Shelton went on. "Friedrich Nietzsche. I stabbed three people to death."

"What monster did you fight?" Mac asked.

Kyle Shelton said nothing. After a long pause, he hung up.

Almost immediately the cell phone in Mac's hand began to vibrate quietly. Mac and Rufus went to the front door and stepped out. When the door was closed, Mac answered the call. Danny told him what he had found on Shelton's blog.

"I followed up and guess what I found?" said Danny.

Mac guessed. He was right.

"You want me there?" asked Danny.

"I want you to get at least eight hours of sleep," answered Mac.

Mac closed his cell phone and said, "It's time, Rufus."

Stella's cell phone rang and someone buzzed her apartment at the same time.

She popped her phone open and moved to the door to buzz her visitor in without asking who it was. She knew who it was.

Before he got up the elevator and to her door, Aiden had filled her in.

"Warrant?" asked Stella.

"This late?" asked Aiden. "It'll take too long.

Let's hope he feels like being cooperative. If not, I'll wait there while Flack tracks down a judge who's awake and having a good day. You going to meet us there?"

Now there was a knock at the door.

"It's yours," said Stella. "Someone's knocking at my door."

She hung up, checked the pocket of her loose jeans, resisted the urge to tuck in her blue blouse, and opened the door.

"Agent Harbaugh, I presume?" she asked. "Right on time."

He was wearing a dark suit and tie, the FBI uniform. He was tall and older than she would have guessed from his voice on the phone. His neatly cut hair was white. His skin was weathered less from age than from the sun. He was definitely good looking.

"Come in," Stella said.

He did. She closed the door. There was no need for him to look at the paintings on the wall. He had looked at each one carefully the last time he was here.

"Would you like that Coke?" Stella asked.

"No, thanks. May I?" he asked, nodding at a chair.

"Please," said Stella.

He sat. She sat across from him.

He looked at her with a sad smile and sat back. He had come to kill her, but there was no hurry.

*   *   *

The shop was dark except for two low-wattage night-lights inside.

Flack knocked and looked at Aiden, who shifted the weight of her kit. Flack knocked again harder, much harder. The door rattled. If there were a sensitive alarm it would have gone off by now, but they heard nothing.

Flack didn't give up. More than two minutes passed before they could make out the figure of a man coming down the stairs inside the shop.

Arvin Bloom stopped for an instant at the bottom of the stairs, recognizing the police officers, and then, with what looked like a huge sigh that shook his body, he came to the door and opened it.

"We'd like to take another look at some of your furniture," said Aiden.

"Now?" said Bloom. "You are harassing me. Do you have a warrant?"

"No," said Flack, "but we can get one. Same deal as before. One of us gets the warrant. The other stays with you. How do you want it?"

"Come in," said Bloom, stepping aside. "I'd ask you to be fast if I thought it would do any good."

Flack and Aiden entered. Bloom closed the door behind them and made no move to turn on more light.

Flack stayed with Bloom and Aiden went into the darkness at the back of the shop. She was back in five minutes, saying, "The bloodwood cabinet. Where is it?"

"Sold, this afternoon," said Bloom. "I made a good sale. If I'd waited, I could have done better, but I wanted to get money back to the widow of Asher Glick, *aleviah sholom.*"

"Who bought the bloodwood cabinet?" Aiden asked.

"A couple," said Bloom. "Maybe in their late fifties. Dressed like money. Handed me cash, $25,000. They didn't want a receipt and they had a van parked illegally in front of the shop. I helped them put the cabinet in the van."

"So you don't have a name or address for these customers?" asked Flack.

Bloom shook his head "no" and said, "It's not unusual."

"Where's the money?" asked Aiden.

"Got to the bank before it closed," he said. "You can check with the bank in the morning. I didn't kill Asher."

"We will," said Aiden, starting toward the door. Flack wanted to keep Bloom talking, but Aiden was now on the street, so Flack followed her, closing the door behind him.

"What's up?" he asked her.

They both looked through the window at Bloom, who looked back at them. Aiden and Flack moved toward their car.

"I picked up what looked like fresh latent prints on the wall the bloodwood cabinet was against. Two different sets."

"One Bloom's," said Flack. "The other the customer who bought the cabinet."

"Or the person who helped Bloom get it out of his shop," she said. "One more thing."

As they walked Aiden pulled a see-through packet out of her pocket and held it up for him to see.

"What is it?" asked Flack.

"Sawdust," said Aiden, smiling.

FBI Agent Harbaugh sat comfortably, legs crossed in the chair facing Stella.

"I like the paintings," he said, looking around the room. "That's an Andre Danton, isn't it?"

The painting he was looking at on the wall behind Stella was a scene of a narrow cobblestone street with houses seeming to bow toward the lone old woman on the sidewalk with a kerchief over her head and a basket of flowers under her arm.

"Yes," said Stella, without turning to look at the painting.

She examined Harbaugh again. He was lean, sat straight and was in obvious good shape, but she could see now from the age spots on his hands, the hair growing on his ears, that he was at least in his mid-sixties. His teeth were white, even and definitely his own. His face was weathered, the stereo-typed image of a cowboy.

"Yes," he said, seeing the question in her eyes. "I'm a temporary retread, brought back as a consultant because this guy was mine until I retired. Nine people over a fifteen-year period. Texas, California, Illinois, Tampa. Stopped three years before my retirement."

Stella nodded, hands folded in her lap.

"Pattern," said Harbaugh. "Kills three. Gets his fix and goes underground till he has to start again."

"The crucifix? The victims? The words in Hebrew?" asked Stella.

Harbaugh shrugged and said, "All of his victims have been religious, not just Jewish. I think the last one in this cycle will be a Christian minister or a Catholic priest."

"Just a hunch?" asked Stella.

"Fits the previous pattern," he said.

"Is any of that true?" she asked.

For a few seconds they both sat silently and then Stella reached into the lacquered red box on the table next to her. She pulled out a small gun and a bottle and held them up for him to see.

The bottle was the antihistamine syrup from Stella's bathroom cabinet. The gun was her .38, and it was aimed at him.

"You were careful," she said, "but you moved a few things, not much, but enough for me to notice. A lot of my job is to notice small things."

"You think I moved your pill bottles?" he said.

"I know you did," she said.

He nodded, now understanding, and said, "Fingerprints."

"And two strands of hair in my bathroom drain where you poured the poison into my antihistamine bottle."

The man remained rigid, eyes on Stella.

"You're not and never were in the FBI," she said. "Your name is George Melvoy. You were born in Des Moines seventy-three years ago. You were a medic, an infantry corporal with MacArthur when he landed in Korea in 1950. After the war you went to Iowa State University, majored in pharmacy. You've had your own successful drugstore in Des Moines for more than forty years. Wife died six years ago. No children. I've got a photograph of you faxed from the *Des Moines Register* four hours ago."

Melvoy didn't move.

"You're losing hair," she said.

"Yes," he said.

"You know why?" asked Stella.

"Yes," he said.

Stella nodded and said, "Aluminum levels in your hair are high. The DNA we got from your hair shows three tiny abnormalities on some of your chromosomes, abnormalities that may be a sign of Alzheimer's."

" 'Tough old bird,' " he said, almost to himself. "And 'sharp.' That's what my customers say. In a year or so I'll be a grinning, helpless rag doll who doesn't recognize anyone. Well, I don't plan to be around when that starts happening. I'm glad you didn't use that medicine. It was a coward's way of killing."

"A capful wouldn't have killed me," she said. She had couriered the syrup over to the lab earlier, had them run an emergency analysis on the doctored syrup. "It might have made me sick. It would take the whole bottle to kill and even then it wouldn't be a certainty."

Melvoy shook his head and said, "Good thing I'm retired. I could probably kill a customer with a wrong prescription."

Stella put the bottle back in the open box on the table.

"Why didn't you arrest me when you found out?" he asked.

"I want to know why you want to kill me," she said.

"Don't anymore. I did when I walked through that door, but . . . Remember Matthew Heath?" he asked.

"Tall, thin, red hair, worked in the lab for a few months," she said. "He had a seizure. When he came back from the hospital, he was wearing thick glasses and found he couldn't look at the computer screen for more than a minute or two before he felt a seizure coming on. He just quit one day. I heard he was going to cooking school."

Melvoy was shaking his head "no" and said, "Matt went to a cooking school in Switzerland someplace. I paid. Matt's grandfather was my best friend. You've heard of the USS *Walke*?"

"Saw it on your cap in the videotapes at the two crime scenes," she said.

"Matt's grandfather died when the *Walke* was hit off the coast of Korea. He had one son and the son had one son, Matt. When Matt's parents died, the boy came to live with me. At the end, we were the only family we had."

"The end?" prompted Stella.

"Matt shot himself. At first I was angry with him for doing that to me, leaving me alone. Then I was relieved, relieved of the responsibility of propping him up. Then came the guilt. I loved the boy."

Melvoy laughed.

"Yes?" asked Stella.

"You're the first person I said that to," he said. "Never said it to Matt. Said it a few dozen times maybe to my wife. Saying 'I love you' doesn't come easy in my family."

He pulled himself together and sat up straight, letting out a deep breath and saying, "Ask it."

Stella knew what he meant.

"Why did you want to kill me?"

"Because you killed Matt," he said. "A good, happy kid who wanted nothing more than to please you. He wanted to be like you. Worked days without sleeping. Started to get headaches. Doctors warned him, told him to get another job. I told the boy I'd take him on as my partner and leave the drugstore to him when I died. Turned me down, talked about you. You never told him he was doing a good job, never encouraged him, kept pointing out the mistakes he was making."

Stella knew there was definitely some truth in what the man was saying, but there was also some ignorance.

"That's the way we work," said Stella. "It was the way I was treated when I started with the CSI unit. We see things, do things no one should have to see or do."

"And you like it," said Melvoy with a challenge.

"Yes," said Stella. "But it was the wrong career choice for Matt."

"He stayed with it because he wanted your approval," said Melvoy. "And it killed him."

There wasn't much more for Stella to say, at least nothing that would help the man across from her. Melvoy's face had gone slack and his eyes were focused somewhere in the past.

Stella had treated Matthew Heath exactly as she had treated at least a dozen other incoming lab techs before him, lab techs who aspired to be in the field. The strong and the smart made it, many of them moving to other cities where there were jobs a step up on the forensic ladder. Stella had been sure the second day he was on the job that Matthew Heath was not going to make it, that the longer he stayed the more the job would get to him.

Melvoy forced himself back into the present, stood and began to reach into his pocket.

"Don't," said Stella firmly, the service revolver in her hand.

Melvoy slowly slid a small spiral-bound note-book from his pocket.

"I fill these things all the time now," he said. "Have a drawer full of them. I write down just about everything I have to do."

He flipped open the notebook, turned it so Stella could see the large block letters: KILL STELLA BONASERA.

"You're going to have to shoot me. Now's as good a time as any, just be sure to shoot to kill."

He put the notebook back in his pocket and stood.

"No," she said.

"For the past few months I've been having short blackouts, loss of memory. It's starting."

He closed the distance between them and Stella stood. "I won't shoot to kill," she said. "And I don't think you'll hurt me."

"I'm tired," said Melvoy, sitting again, eyes closed. "I'll make a trade."

"A trade?" asked Stella.

"I tell you who the next crucifixion target is and you shoot me," he said. "You a good shot?"

"Yes," she said.

"Deal?" he asked.

"No deal," she said.

"Didn't think so," he said with a sigh. "I can see why Matt wanted to be like you. Okay, I was watching you at the second crime scene. A priest in black, white collar, walked behind the crowd. I glanced at him. He looked at the storefront and crossed himself. When he walked past, a man at the rear of the crowd moved after him; only saw the back of him but he was definitely following the priest. Later, when the body was taken away, I went in the direction of the priest and the man who had followed him."

"Why?" asked Stella.

"Had the idea that if I came up with something I could get close to you."

"No," she said. "There's something else."

He didn't answer.

"You're a Catholic," she said.

"Was," he said.

"So am I," she said. "You wanted to protect the priest."

"I don't know," said Melvoy. "God, I'm tired."

"The priest," Stella prompted.

"Father William Wosak," said Melvoy. "Parish priest at St. Martine's. Sometimes I think there is a God. I've got the feeling that he stopped me from killing you. I'm really glad I didn't."

"So am I," said Stella. "You're a combat veteran. The Veterans Administration will take care of you."

"I've got enough money and nobody to give it to but doctors," he said. "But I meant what I said. I don't intend to be here when it gets worse. I intend to commit a mortal sin."

Stella said nothing. The decision was his. She couldn't stop him and maybe, given his pride, it wasn't an unreasonable choice to make.

"Could you recognize the person who followed the priest?" she asked.

"No," he said. "His back was to me. He was tall, heavyset, wore a dark blue shirt with short sleeves. My money's going to Alzheimer's research. It's all arranged. Now you better go save a priest."

Stella took out her cell phone, moved to the window and made her call. She kept her gun in her hand and didn't turn her back on Melvoy, whose eyes were closed, mouth open, head back against the chair.

He moved quickly. Stella was in the middle of a sentence. Before she could reach him, Melvoy had taken the antihistamine syrup bottle from the box, opened it with a quick twist and gulped the thick liquid down. He handed Stella the empty bottle.

"Don't call for help," he said, moving back to the chair.

"I have to," said Stella.

Stella dialed 911, identified herself and asked for an ambulance. When she turned off the phone, Melvoy was having minor convulsions.

Jane Parsons brushed a strand of hair from her forehead, popped the two aspirin into her mouth and washed them down with room-temperature bottled water. She had a headache and may or may not have been hungry. She wasn't sure.

She checked the clock on the wall of the lab. Ten forty-five. She had been working for the past four-teen hours.

Her time had not been wasted. After examining the DNA sample Aiden had given her, Jane had gone to the Internet and followed link after link, most of them leading nowhere, all of them interest-ing. She had also sent eight e-mails and made four phone calls.

The rough draft of her report was on the screen in front of her. She scrolled down, being sure that she couched her conclusions with protective phrases, including: "It appears to be," "Research at the following laboratories and universities supports the conclusion that . . ." and "Therefore, it is almost certain that . . ."

When she was reasonably satisfied with the report, she printed four copies, one for Aiden, one for Stella, one for Flack and one for Mac. They'd have them in the morning.

She stood up, moved the mouse and put the computer to sleep. It needed the rest. She screwed the cap back on the water bottle.

DNA did not lie. It did speak a foreign language, which Jane had been taught to read with reasonable fluency. In her mind, there was no doubt. The person whose DNA she examined had lied.

Why the lie? Jane didn't know. That was a job for the Crime Scene Investigator in charge of the case, Stella.

Jane looked around, almost-empty bottle in hand, took off her lab coat and draped it on the chair, walked to the door and turned off the lights.

The thought came to her fleetingly. She realized it wasn't the first time. What was the relationship between Mac and Stella? All business? Friends? Something more? It really wasn't Jane's business and normally she saved her curiosity for the secrets the microscopic strands of DNA could reveal. Each day she learned something new. Some days she discovered something new.

Mac's office was dark. She didn't look at it as she headed for the elevator, deciding that she was more hungry than she was tired. Whatever was in the refrigerator or pantry would have to do.

*   *   *

"Find 'em," said Mac.

There was enough light from the street lamps and the almost-full moon for Mac and Rufus to make their way up the stairs, past the room where the Vorhees massacre had taken place, and into the room of Jacob Vorhees, where Mac took separate pieces of cloth from two evidence bags. He placed the first piece of cloth in front of Rufus, who smelled it and began to move around the room. He picked up Jacob Vorhees' scent almost everywhere. Then Mac placed the second piece of cloth in front of Rufus, who turned, bent his head to the floor and immediately moved to the partially opened closet door. Mac followed, paper bag in hand. Mac pushed the door open and reached up to pull the chain that turned on the hundred-watt bulb in the ceiling.

Mac took out his flashlight and pointed it upward.

"Jacob," he said. "My name is Mac Taylor. I'm with the police."

No response.

"You must be hungry. I've brought sandwiches, an egg salad, a tuna salad and a chicken salad. Choice is yours."

Still no response.

Mac looked at Rufus, who continued to look up at the ceiling inside the closet.

"We'll wait here till you make up your mind,"

said Mac. "But I don't see that you have much of a choice."

It took about two minutes. Mac was sitting on the bed when he heard the sliding sound. He moved to the closet and looked up. A wooden panel was moving, revealing darkness behind it and then the face of Jacob Vorhees. The face was dirty. A red bump stood out on his left cheek. His thick glasses were smudged.

The boy looked down at Rufus and Mac and saw something reassuring in Mac's face. The space in the ceiling was small, but there was enough room for the boy to ease his way through it, put a hand on the hanger rod and drop gently to the floor.

"Show me your badge?" said Jacob.

Mac removed it from his pocket and held it up. In his years on the job three people had actually examined the badge. Jacob Vorhees was the fourth. When he was reasonably satisfied, the boy nodded and Mac put the badge away.

Jacob was wearing faded blue jeans, a pair of Nike shoes with no socks, and a loose-fitting blue T-shirt that needed cleaning. His arms, neck and face were spotted with red bumps. Jacob knew what Mac was looking at and said, "Bugs up there. Lots of them. I kept killing them but they kept coming. Rats too, but they didn't bite, just ran past me or even over me."

Rufus moved next to the boy and rubbed against

his leg. Jacob looked at Mac for permission. Mac nodded and the boy reached down to pet the dog and said, "Bloodhound."

"His name is Rufus," said Mac. "Let's go down to the kitchen and have a sandwich."

When they got to the kitchen and Mac turned on the light, Jacob said, "Tuna."

"Tuna," Mac repeated, removing a wrapped sandwich from the bag he was carrying. He handed it to Jacob.

They sat at the table. Mac took the chicken salad, unwrapped it, removed the top slice of bread before putting it on the floor for Rufus, who was waiting patiently.

"Some of those sores on your arms and neck are infected," said Mac. "We'll stop at the hospital on the way back."

"Am I going to prison?" asked Jacob, before taking a bite of sandwich.

"Tell me what happened," said Mac.

Jacob understood. He finished the mouthful of sandwich, adjusted his glasses, looked up and began.

Joshua walked down the dark street, passing a few people, determined. He came to the steps of St. Martine's, went up and tried to open the door. It was locked. On the wall to the left of the door was a button. Joshua pushed it. Nothing. He pushed it again and kept pushing till someone inside opened the door.

Father Wosak was in sweatpants and a Fordham T-shirt. He wore sandals.

"I want to talk," said Joshua.

The priest saw the clenched fists, the tight jaw of his visitor and stepped back to let him in. Then the priest closed the door.

There were a few dim lights, enough to see by, enough to walk down the aisle toward the altar, where a crucified Christ was illuminated by a small yellow light at his feet. Joshua moved quickly, the priest following him.

Joshua stepped up on the low platform, disappeared for an instant behind the statue and found the tote bag just where he had been told it would be. He unzipped the bag, reached in, came up with a sharpened iron bolt, put it back, came up with a heavy-headed hammer, reached in again and came up with a thick piece of white chalk. He held each item up for the priest to see. Finally he came up with a small gun, which he held in his right hand and pointed at the priest.

"Kneel," said Joshua, bag in one hand, gun in the other.

"No," said Father Wosak. "If you plan to shoot and crucify me, I will not cooperate. I will pray." The priest had clasped his hands and added, "Pray with me in the name of Christ our savior."

"Hypocrite," said Joshua.

"And what does that make you?" said the priest. "You preach. You pray. You murder. Why are you doing this?"

"You know," said Joshua, aiming the gun at the man before him.

"No, I don't," said Father Wosak.

Joshua shook his head. He didn't know how much time he had. There was no time for discussion. This was a Jesuit. If Joshua let him talk, answered his questions, he would be caught up in an explanation, a discussion of religious ethics he would almost certainly lose. No time.

"I didn't lock the door," said the priest. "I pretended to. Someone could walk in any time."

Joshua willed himself not to panic. He stepped closer to the priest, aiming at his chest.

The door to the church did open, with a bang. Flack, Aiden, Stella and two uniformed police officers, all with weapons in hand, stepped in.

"Put it down," Flack called out to Joshua.

Aiden had taken the call from Stella, the call that told her that the man who had called himself Harbaugh had followed a man who had been stalking the priest.

"You don't understand," Joshua said. "This has to be."

"No it doesn't," said Flack, gun aimed straight, held in two hands.

Father Wosak was no more than three feet from Joshua. He held out his right hand. The gun in Joshua's hand was now aimed at the priest's head.

"God is not speaking to you," the priest said. "It's a devil or a demon."

"You believe in devils and demons?" asked Joshua.

"They live inside our heads. They speak to some of us, tell lies. But not often. Usually the voices we hear are our own in disguise."

Joshua laughed. The police had moved forward. Flack was sure he could take Joshua out with one shot.

"Does God also live in my head?" asked Joshua.

"Joshua, God lives in our heads, our bodies, the universe."

"And he speaks to you?" asked Joshua.

"Not in words."

Joshua handed the gun to the priest. Flack, Aiden and the two policemen moved forward with Aiden, who said, "Don't touch that bag. Father, put the gun down on the bench next to you."

The priest did, and turned to put his hand gently on Joshua's shoulder. Joshua wept.

10

JACOB VORHEES LOOKED DOWN AT THE KITCHEN TABLE and softly, without hesitation, said, "I was sleeping. I heard a noise from Becky's room. It was different from the other noises on other nights. I knew Kyle sometimes came through her window and they had sex. Sometimes she made a little noise. None of my business, but this was different. I got up and went down the hallway to Becky's room. I saw my father going in. When I got to Becky's door I saw it. Becky was on the floor. Kyle was on top of her. He had a knife and was stabbing her. My mother was on his back trying to stop him. Kyle was going crazy. I should have done something but I just stood there. Kyle stopped stabbing Becky, pushed my mother off of him and began stabbing her. Then my dad came in and went to help my mom and Becky. Kyle got up and ran at my dad with the knife. I ran out of the room."

"What were you wearing?" asked Mac.

"Wearing? I slept in my clothes. A lot of the time I fall asleep in my clothes."

"Your shoes?"

"I guess I was wearing them too," said the boy. "I don't remember. I just kept thinking, 'He's going to come and kill me next.' I ran downstairs to the garage, got my bike and started pedaling fast, getting away."

"You didn't think about going to a neighbor?" asked Mac.

"He was right behind me. I knew it. I could feel it. I just kept riding. Cars, a truck maybe went by. I think I was heading for the police station or the all-night gas station or the hospital. Then I heard him behind me, looked back. I drove off the road before he could run me over. Got scratched up, crawled into some bushes. I could hear Kyle coming after me. Then I saw the light, Kyle's flashlight. I got the crazy idea of taking off my clothes, dropping them on the way toward town, making him think that was where I was going."

"Why would he think you were taking off your clothes?" asked Mac.

"I don't know. I couldn't think of anything else. But it worked. I ran back here."

"Naked," said Mac.

"Yes," said the boy.

"Why didn't you call the police when you got back?"

"I thought Kyle might be right behind me," he said. "I closed my eyes when I passed Becky's room. I didn't want to see her and my mom laid out on the bed. I could smell the blood. I climbed up into the space over my closet. Even there I could smell the blood."

"Did Kyle come back looking for you?"

"Yes. I could hear him."

"He came in your room?"

"Yes. I could hear him moving around. I think he looked under the bed and I know he opened the closet door and turned on the light. I didn't cry till he was gone."

"Why didn't you come down when the police came?"

"I was afraid Kyle would find out and kill me. I just wanted to hide a few more days and then run away."

The boy was shaking. He was pale, sallow cheeked, filthy and covered with insect bites. Rufus sat next to him.

"He likes you," said Mac.

Jacob looked down at the dog and reached out a hand to pet him.

"You like dogs?" asked Mac.

"Some," said the boy. "Some scare me."

"Rufus is very friendly," said Mac. "Almost all bloodhounds are."

"He smells bad," said Jacob. "He stinks."

"Bloodhounds smell bad, especially when they're wet, which is why you don't see them at dog shows. Ever been to a dog show?"

"Seen one on television."

"It's better live," said Mac. "You sense it. The pride, training, grooming of the dogs."

The boy wasn't really listening. His hand rested on the head of the dog, whose eyes were closed in pleasure at the human touch. After he saw to taking care of the boy's injuries, he would make an appointment with a psychologist, hopefully Sheila Hellyer.

"Jacob," he said.

The boy looked up.

"Did you memorize what you just told me?"

The boy didn't answer. He took his hand from the dog's head and sat upright.

"Most of it wasn't true, was it?" asked Mac.

No answer from Jacob, whose eyes met Mac's and then turned away.

"That's the way it happened," the boy finally said without conviction.

Couldn't have, thought Mac. The boy had been through enough. He should be cleaned up, his wounds cared for and someone found who could comfort him. We'll go over it again in the morning, Mac thought, and see if we can get it right.

It was after midnight.

While she was waiting for the paramedics to arrive at her apartment, Stella had called in for an emergency department vehicle to pick her up immediately. When it arrived, she had simply told the uniformed officer behind the wheel where they were going.

The driver's last name was Fannon. When Stella told him that they were heading for St. Martine's Church in Brooklyn and a priest might be in danger, Fannon had made a serious attempt to break the sound barrier.

When George Melvoy had taken the poison, Stella had acted instantly. She knew the principle poison was turpentine. She had ipecac in her bathroom cabinet, but Stella knew that with turpentine poisoning vomiting should not be induced. Instead she gave him sips of water to ease the burning in his throat.

Stella helped the man off the chair. He resisted, but he was weak now and breathing hard. The convulsions were stronger now. She led him to the bathroom and sat him on the floor next to the tub.

Melvoy gagged twice, leaned over and spewed out a thick greenish spray of liquid that splattered in the tub. She held his head as he convulsed in pain again, that which he most prized, his dignity, now gone.

When the paramedics had arrived, Stella had held the hand of the man who had planned to kill her. The hand was dappled with age spots and his face looked as old as he really was.

At the hospital, they would probably place a tube down Melvoy's nose and into his stomach, a nasogastric tube, to wash out his stomach. He would be treated with activated charcoal and examined with an endoscopy, the placement of a camera down the throat, to determine the extent of the burns to the esophagus and stomach. IV fluids would be given. If the treatment worked, there could still be extensive damage to the mouth, throat and stomach. Damage might continue for weeks. He might recover and he might die in pain a month later. A hard way to die.

Now Stella sat across from Joshua in the same room at CSI headquarters where they had sat before. Aiden was working on the contents of the tote bag and Flack was in the next room listening. They had decided that Joshua would be more likely to talk to a single person. Stella, after a cup of thick, terrible tasting coffee, had volunteered.

Stella remembered that she would have to clean Melvoy's vomit off her tub. It might take a while. It would be hard and she would have to work at getting rid of the foul acrid odor. She had seen worse, worked with worse, but not in her own home.

"You won't believe me," said Joshua. "My faith is being tested."

"Try," said Stella.

Joshua looked tired. He leaned forward, hands

clasped. He wore black Dockers, a gray polo shirt
and sneakers. He sighed deeply and said, "The priest
killed Glick and Joel Besser."

"Why?"

"They were Jews," said Joshua. "That's enough."

"Why the shooting and the crucifixion?"

Joshua shook his head.

"Anti-Semites have tortured Jews, crucified
Jews, for over two thousand years. Yeshua was one
of thousands of Jews crucified."

"How do you know he killed Glick and Besser?"

"Got a phone call," Joshua said. "Man with a heavy
Spanish accent said he had found something and was
afraid to go to the police. He told me where it was and
said he thought his priest was a murderer. He was crying. I tried to ask him more but he hung up."

He lifted his head and faced Stella.

"You don't believe me," he said.

"Go on," Stella said.

"I went to the church," Joshua said. "I went behind the altar, behind the statue of Yeshua, and
there it was."

"The bag," said Stella.

"Yes."

"You hadn't put it there earlier?"

"No."

"You had the gun in your hand when we came,"
said Stella. "Were you going to shoot Father
Wosak?"

"I wanted to stop him from killing more Jews."

"That's not an answer," said Stella.

"I don't know what I was going to do, but it doesn't matter. You came. Here I am and you don't believe me."

Aiden opened the door and nodded at Stella, who got up. Flack came into the room to continue the interrogation. In the hallway, Aiden said, "I haven't had time to go over everything, but I can tell you that the hammer in the bag is probably the same one used to crucify the two victims. I found traces of iron oxide on the head. It matches the bolts used in the crucifixions. The only prints on the handle are Joshua's."

"But?" said Stella, seeing that Aiden had more to tell her.

"Joshua's fingerprints are on two of the bolts and on the gun," said Aiden. "No other prints. No prints on the other two bolts."

"Could he have been wearing gloves?" said Stella.

"Then why touch the bolts with his bare hands in the church? Why handle the hammer bare-handed in the church? There are no gloves in his pockets or in the bag. And the bolts are all wrong. They're not sharpened. They're almost blunt. Hammering them through flesh and into the floor would have been nearly impossible."

"So," said Stella. "Joshua might be telling the truth. Which means he was set up."

"Which doesn't tell us why," said Aiden. "I'm going back to the tote bag."

And, thought Stella, I'm going to look for a man with a thick Spanish accent. She had the feeling that the accent had not been real. She also had the feeling that the man himself might not be real.

Joshua would have a long night in jail.

At two a.m. Danny Messer awoke in the darkness of his bedroom, sat up sweating and fumbled for his glasses on the table next to the bed.

Something was different. He clicked on the light and looked at his hands. The tremor was completely gone. His first reaction was relief. This was followed almost immediately by fear, fear that it would come back.

It was clear to him now. Maybe it had always been clear. His grandfather and his father had both become police officers to face their fear. They had been good, honest, often decorated and well respected. There had never been any question about Danny becoming a cop. It was a given. Danny understood. He had acknowledged the fear and now he sat up in his bed and wondered if he had chosen CSI because it was relatively safe but would still allow him to carry on the Messer tradition. Were the street fights he had been in growing up, the drug dealers he had stood up to, gangbangers he had refused to back away from and even sought out, part of the pattern of facing his fear?

At this point, it didn't matter. He was who he was and was dedicated to and fascinated by his job. He wondered if he would tell all this to Sheila Hellyer. Probably.

He got up, moved to his computer, pressed a button on the keyboard and pulled up the on-screen version of the report he had given Mac on the Vorhees murder. He read it carefully, trying to make sense of what he saw, and then came up with a theory. In the morning, he would share his thoughts with Mac. In the morning he would find out that Mac had come to the same conclusion he had. Kyle Shelton had not murdered the Vorhees family. They would have to go back to the computer and create a new virtual reality scenario.

Danny put his computer to sleep, went to the kitchen for a bottled water and went back to bed. He placed the bottle on the table next to the bed, checked his hands again to be sure they were not shaking, put his glasses on the table and turned off the light. He was asleep almost instantly.

It was 2:15 in the morning.

Stella stirred and came awake. She got out of the chair and moved to the side of the hospital bed.

There was some light from the slightly open door of the bathroom. She could see George

Melvoy's tube-connected face, could hear him breathe. The breathing was shallow, with a painful sandpapery rasp. The monitor, however, bouncing with mountains being painted by green light, showed that his vital signs were steady. The man was strong.

Stella ran her fingers through her hair and touched his arm. She liked the man who had tried to kill her. In the morning she would tell him that he had almost certainly saved a life. She wasn't yet certain whose life he had saved.

She appreciated the irony. Because this man had stalked her, planned to kill her, he had seen something that led to the saving of a life.

She didn't know where she had heard or read it, but the words came back to her as they had in the past. It was a kind of non-prayer: Lord, if you'll forgive the little tricks I've done to you, I'll forgive the great big one you've done to me.

Satisfied that Melvoy was all right, Stella went back to the aluminum-armed chair and sat. The chair wasn't made for comfort but for brief visits to the ill. For visitors of the dying, more comfortable chairs would magically appear.

Joshua had broken down in the church and Father Wosak had moved to put his arm around and comfort the man. In the morning, she would let Flack take the lead interrogating Joshua. Stella would sit in.

Before she left the hospital, she wanted to talk to Melvoy. She had decided not to talk to him about Matthew Heath, the lab assistant who had taken his own life. If Stella had contributed to his suicide, the contribution had been infinitesimal. It wasn't Stella with whom he could not cope. It was the world that had been too much for Matthew Heath. She saw that now. Perhaps she should have seen signs of it when the boy had dutifully, but with no signs of developing skill, gone through the day.

She wasn't going to talk about that with George Melvoy.

The clock in the window of the coffee shop across the street read 2:37 a.m.

Kyle Shelton sat in the window, glancing at the clock and the few people of the night who passed by the night-lit interiors of the shops. There was a young laughing couple, arm in arm. He thought of Becky and closed his eyes. There was a trio of young men whispering, emitting danger. Kyle could sense it.

The air conditioner in the window next to the one before which he was sitting rattled and gave off spurts of almost cool air. The night heat seeped through the windows, the walls.

He had gone through cycles about his plan. Sometimes he thought that for something improvised, it was reasonably good. Things could go wrong, but it should hold. At other times, he was certain it had been a terrible plan, that the CSI cop Taylor was gathering pinpricks of evidence, secrets of blood and DNA, fingerprints he had forgotten.

His friend Scott Shuman said Kyle could crash at his apartment for a few nights. Scott was a good guy who was taking a big chance harboring a fugitive. Kyle had known Scott—short, dark unkempt curly black hair, slightly pudgy—in college. Both had been philosophy majors. They had become friends. Scott had become a well-paid computer program designer for an Indian company that explored the universe. Scott had never married. Though they never discussed it, Kyle thought his friend was probably gay but hadn't yet admitted it to himself. Kyle could be wrong. He had been wrong about many things.

Middle of the night. Kyle felt it coming. He was going to allow himself to grieve. Actually, he had no choice. He could feel it happening.

Kyle could not remember crying as he was about to do, shaking with grief and loss, considering that there might really be a malevolent force that lived and thrived on the pain of humans. He wept and remembered Ovid's words: "Suppressed grief suffocates. It rages within the breast and is forced to multiply its strength."

The clock in the coffeehouse window read 2:49 a.m.

* * *

Mac's watch read 2:49 a.m. He was walking Rufus to the small dog park five blocks from his apartment. He should have returned the dog before coming home. Mac had long ago admitted that his one emotional weakness was dogs. He knew how to handle them, work with them, admire them. He also knew he did not want to own one in the city, not with his job.

There was another single figure, a man, in the dog park. He sat across from Mac on a wooden bench and watched his short-legged pug waddle around the grass and dirt. The man, in his forties or fifties, looked tired. His arms were draped over the bench and he eyed Mac and Rufus warily. This was Manhattan, the middle of the night.

Rufus and the pug walked slowly up to each other, sniffed and then stepped away to take care of their own business.

Then Rufus moved to the man on the bench, sniffed and hurried back to Mac, who reached down, petted him and whispered, "I know."

The man on the other bench was carrying something that Rufus had been taught to detect and report. It could be drugs or a gun. In spite of the heat that had bled into the night, Mac wore a light jacket under which were his holster and gun.

He had decided that the man with the pug was almost certainly not a threat. He was a man with a dog.

Mac thought about his wife, Claire, again. His

thoughts of grief were not that different from those of Kyle Shelton, though he didn't put them in the words of a philosopher.

A hot night like this back in Chicago, coming back from the wedding of Claire's cousin. Too much to drink but happy, comforted by her closeness. They had walked instead of going home, talked instead of sleeping, made plans instead of accepting the need for sleep. It had been a good night. There had been many of them. Not enough of them.

Mac got up. The man on the bench watched him leave, his pug rubbing against his leg.

In a few hours, he would find Kyle Shelton. In a few hours he would talk to Jacob Vorhees again. In a few hours the investigation of the murder of the Vorhees family would be over, but it would not be the end of the horror for the boy and the young man who liked to quote philosophers.

Mac looked at his watch: 3:20 a.m.

It was 3:20 a.m.

Sak Pyon looked at the illuminated dial of the clock on the bedside table. He carefully peeled back the sheet, sat up slowly and got out of bed, moving softly across the floor toward the bathroom. He did not want to disturb his sleeping wife.

Nothing like this had happened in at least five years, maybe more. He slept without an alarm clock and woke automatically at 4:15 a.m. every day. He got washed, brushed his teeth and hair, dressed and left the apartment without making a sound. He would pick up coffee and a fresh blueberry muffin before he got to the shop.

Because he was early and because he had much to think about, Pyon decided to walk to work. The young policeman would probably be back about the sketch Pyon had drawn, a sketch not of the man who had gone through his shop and almost certainly killed the strange Jewish boy next door. Only last night before he had fallen asleep did he realize that he had drawn a stand-up comedian from one of the television shows he had seen on the Comedy Network. The policeman would almost certainly be back.

Pyon kept walking, the day already pre-dawn muggy. In Korea, the summer heat had not bothered him, but a quarter of a century in New York had changed him.

He thought of the man he should have sketched, should have told the policeman about, but Pyon had remembered the moment when the other man had entered the store and moved to the counter and leaned over, invading Pyon's space, eyes unblinking as he quietly said, "I have your home address and the home address in Hartford of your daughter. Your granddaughter's name is Anna. She's five."

Pyon nodded, afraid that he understood what he was being told.

"I have not been here today," the man said. "If you tell anyone, the police, your wife, your daughter, anyone, I will kill your family. Do you believe me?"

Pyon believed the man, who hovered over him with a look much like that of the militia officer who had killed Pyon's father with a single shot to the head, killed him calmly in front of the family. Pyon believed this man.

And so he had lied to the policeman and made a sketch of a television actor whose name he did not know. Pyon, as he approached the shop on the still-darkened street, gave serious consideration to quietly selling the shop to one of the several people who had shown interest. He could sell the shop, pack and . . . no. The man would find him. He would certainly know where to find Pyon's daughter, Tina, who lived in Hartford with her husband and Pyon's granddaughter. The man would find them. Of this he was sure.

Perhaps the oddest thing about the threat delivered by the man, thought Pyon, was the fact that it had been delivered in almost perfect Korean.

He looked at his watch as he turned on the light. It was almost 5:30 a.m. Through the window he could see the coming dawn over the buildings across the street.

*   *   *

At 5:30 a.m., Aiden Burn's radio came on with the news on the half hour. She got up. She was meeting Hawkes at 6:30 a.m. He had left a voice message on her cell phone saying he had reexamined the bodies of the two dead men and had returned to the crime scenes. He had found something interesting.

Stella and Flack would be wearing down Joshua again this morning, but she wasn't sure about him. Evidence led both toward and away from Arvin Bloom. Her report had laid out the pros and cons. Her report did not include her gut feeling.

She was dressed, showered and through the door by six a.m.

At six a.m. Joshua was found in his holding cell by a guard bringing breakfast. Joshua sat still on his cot, palms out, both deeply gashed. Blood drenched the cot and formed a small dark lake on the floor. Joshua's face was white.

The guard, a man named Michael Molton who had twenty-two years of service, put the tray on the floor, called out for help and moved to find something with which he could stop the bleeding. It was only when Adams was bent over and pressing the part of the blanket that wasn't covered with blood against the wounds that he looked down at Joshua's bare feet in a second pool of blood. Both feet also bore gashes like the ones in his palms. On the floor near the cot, the guard saw a bloody piece of rusted metal about the size of a cell phone.

Molton thought he had seen everything, but this was a new one. And, he thought, the day is just starting.

It was six minutes past six in the morning.

11

"THEY LOOK LIKE MOB HITS," said Hawkes, his eyes moving between the two sheet-covered dead men on the tables in front of him. They were turned facedown. "But whoever did it is even better than a mob hit man."

Aiden watched as Hawkes leaned over the body of Asher Glick.

"Two shots, .40 caliber fired from no more than an inch away," Hawkes said. "Found the bullets in the flesh under the tongue, less than half an inch apart. The other one . . ."

He pointed at the body of Besser.

"Same thing. Bullets from the same gun fired about an inch away. Bullets found lodged in the skull over the right temple about an inch apart."

An examination of the bullets from the victims identified them as .40 caliber Smith & Wessons.

They were looking for a pistol, one that could fit in a pocket. They were also looking for a semiautomatic, which would allow the killer to get off two shots quickly. Aiden knew there were pistols no more than five and a half inches long and weighing twenty-two ounces. Aiden told Hawkes.

"Indeed," said Hawkes, "but there was something interesting, which was why I left you the message."

Aiden's eyes were fixed on him.

"Victim one, Glick," said Hawkes, "was standing when he was shot."

"Blood trail a little over three feet from where he fell or was placed," she confirmed.

"Right," said Hawkes. "Victim two was seated."

"Blood spatter on the chair he was sitting in," she said.

"Checked the angle of entry again," said Hawkes. "This time assuming we were dealing with a pro. If he held the gun something like this . . ."

Hawkes stood straight up, hand out as if he were a kid playing war, aimed at Aiden.

"Pretty much standard position," he said.

Aiden agreed.

Hawkes nodded and said, "Your shooter is about six feet four inches tall. Given the angle of the entry on both victims, I got a dummies and put a gun in its hand. Then I found dummies the same height as the two victims."

"And," said Aiden, "given the angle of entry, if the shooter was standing, he had to be tall."

"Six-four is close," said Hawkes. "Got any suspects that tall?"

"Indeed we do," said Aiden.

"Coffee?" asked Hawkes.

"No time," said Aiden. "Later maybe."

"I've got to get Glick's body to the widow today," said Hawkes. "If I don't, there'll be a protest in front of the mayor's office before the day is over."

Aiden headed back to the lab and the computer, but there were some things the Internet probably couldn't tell her. She would have to make some calls.

Mac sat at his desk. He had calls to make too.

He had reluctantly returned Rufus to the dog unit.

Now he sat in front of the screen of his computer, where he had read Danny's e-mail about Kyle Shelton's web site and blog. Mac was looking for what he could find on Shelton's blog. There had been no entry the day before.

It was too early to call the college, but he tried anyway and got through the recorded message to a human being in student housing. Her name was Tara Abbott. She sounded sprightly and asked Mac a few questions to verify who he was. She took his phone number and said she would call him back

instantly. She did. She wanted to confirm that he
was a police officer.

"How long do you keep housing records?" he
asked.

"Forever," she said. "We've got them on disks now,
going back to the founding of the college in 1934."

"Can you find a student named Kyle Shelton?"
Mac asked. "Probably there about five years ago?"

"I can and will," she said.

Joshua looked dead to Flack, but there the man lay
in bed, hands and feet bandaged, blood drained
from his face. He was covered by a sheet and blanket, an IV pole and bag next to him.

"Can you hear me?" asked Flack.

No answer.

"Can you hear me?" he repeated, leaning closer
to Joshua, whose thin breath touched Flack's face.

Flack was about to give up when Joshua's eyes
fluttered and opened in a squint as if blinded by the
light, but the light was dim and the window shade
was down. A brownish muted light filtered through
the shade.

Joshua blinked, looked around without moving
his head and his eyes found the detective.

"Water," Joshua gasped.

Flack got the slightly dusty glass from the table. A
straw protruded from the water. Joshua took a long
sip and gagged. Flack put the water back on the table.

"You want a lawyer?" asked Flack.

"No. I want to die, wanted to die," rasped Joshua. "Only now, I'm afraid."

"Of who?"

"Of what. Of dying. Last night in that cell I lost my faith," said Joshua with a cough. "Is what I did in the newspapers? On the radio?"

"It will be," said Flack.

Joshua sighed.

"I've lost my faith, my congregation, what little reputation I had. Everyone will find out about my drinking. 'Messianic Jewish leader crucifies two Jews, caught while he was about to do the same to a Catholic priest. Attempts to crucify himself in prison.' That's a summary, not a headline."

"Did you kill those men?" Flack asked.

"No. I thought the priest had done it," Joshua said. "The phone call . . ."

His voice trailed off.

"Hispanic accent?" asked Flack, remembering the drawing by Sak Pyon of an Hispanic man.

Joshua tried to nod, but the movement caused pain that was clearly, instantly frozen on his face.

"More water?" asked Flack.

"No," said Joshua.

Flack said nothing as he sat looking at the man, who was breathing hard from the effort of talking.

Flack would not say it. His job wasn't to go on hunches and intuition, but to come up with evi-

dence, find suspects. He thought Joshua was innocent of murder. He may have been guilty of many
other things, but not these murders. Prejudice had
crept in. Flack didn't like it.

His cell phone vibrated in his pocket. Flack took
it out, flipped it open.

"Yes?" said Flack.

"Is he going to pull through?" asked Stella.

"Looks that way," said Flack, looking at Joshua,
whose eyes were again closed. "Says he didn't do
the murders."

"Probably didn't," said Stella. "Step into the hall."

Flack assumed Stella had something private to
say, something she did not want Joshua to hear
Flack's response to. He moved to the door and
stepped out. Stella stood there, closing her phone
and putting it in her pocket.

Stella had spent the last two hours with Melvoy
in a room on the floor below Joshua's. Melvoy was
going to live, but there was a price to pay. His voice
would forever be a rasp and his mouth would be
almost painfully dry. He would have to carry a bottle of water everywhere he went. With Alzheimer's
taking over his mind, he would almost certainly
forget to drink the water.

"What am I being charged with?" Melvoy had
whispered when he saw Stella. Talking hurt, whispering didn't, but he knew it was hard for Stella to
hear him.

The list wasn't long. Attempted murder. Breaking and entering. Threatening the life of a police officer.

But Stella decided she wasn't going to press charges. Melvoy would walk out of the hospital a hero who had helped the police track down a murderer and prevent another killing.

"No more talk for now," Stella said, seeing the pain in his eyes.

"One thing," he whispered.

"Yes?"

"Why are you spending this time with me?"

"I like you," she said.

"Mutual," he managed with a smile.

Stella smiled back.

"Got to go," she said.

He nodded.

She had the number of Joshua's room. When she was outside of Joshua's room minutes later, she heard a familiar voice beyond the door, which was when she had called Flack.

Both Aiden and Danny had spent the better part of two morning hours making calls. Both eventually succeeded, but they weren't sure what their success meant.

Aiden made a call and arranged to meet Stella and Flack at a deli near the lab. Aiden gathered her information and headed for the door.

Danny went to Mac's office, file under his arm.

He knocked and walked in. Mac was hunched over photographs of Jacob Vorhees taken in the hospital. He held up one photo toward Danny and said, "What do you see?"

Danny took the photo. Mac saw that the tremor was gone. The boy was sitting up, arms out, covered with deep, red bug bites. He was sitting with his legs straight out, bottoms of his feet facing the camera.

Danny handed the photo back to Mac, who waited for an answer.

"Bottoms of the feet," said Danny.

Mac nodded his agreement.

"He said he walked more than a mile through woods and yards," said Danny. "There's not a scratch or bruise on his feet."

"He lied," said Mac.

"You know why?"

"Maybe."

The computer on his desk indicated that a message was coming in. The name and number of the caller appeared on the telephone's screen.

Mac nodded for Danny to join him behind the desk.

"Kyle Shelton's parents live in California," said Mac. "He had a sister who died when she was twelve. I called Shelton's parents and left a message asking them to call back."

Mac pushed a button and put the call on speaker-phone.

"Is this Detective Taylor?" a woman asked.

"Yes, ma'am," said Mac. "Could you tell me the names of any friends your son might have in New York?"

"Why?" asked Shelton's mother on the phone with concern.

"We're looking for him," Mac had said. "He's missing. We don't believe anything has happened to him."

"Lord God I hope you're right," she said. "Haven't heard from him in months. You'll let us know when you find him?"

"Yes," Mac had said. "His friends?"

"Not many," she said with a sigh. "He was a lonely boy, studious, paid his own way through college. Always gentle. And then he volunteered for Iraq. He didn't discuss it with us. When he came back, he had changed. He wasn't a boy anymore. He was a man, a man with great dignity and pain. He didn't smile anymore."

"Yes, ma'am," Mac said.

"Kyle's friends in New York," she said. "Well, if there were girls, he never said. In college he roomed with a nice boy, Scott Shuman. They were good friends. I think Scott's still in New York."

The information confirmed what Mac had already learned from the university. Kyle Shelton had roomed with Scott Shuman all through college, first two years in a dorm, last two in an apartment.

Danny had moved to the computer. On the screen was information on Shuman, including his address, phone number and place of employment.

"You'll call or have Kyle call?" the woman said.

"I will," said Mac. "Thank you."

He pushed a button, turning off the phone.

"You've got something?" Mac said.

While the information on Shuman was being printed, Danny handed the file he had brought to Mac, who read slowly and carefully.

Howard Vorhees had an arrest record, not in New York, but in Seattle, Minneapolis and Nashville. All of the arrests, which took place in the last five years, were for sexual advances to under-age girls. All of the girls had been frightened, but hadn't been touched. The police had questioned Vorhees and then let him go with a warning. Soon after each reported sexual advance, the Vorhees family had moved to another city. They had only been in New York for two years.

"Probably more that didn't report him," said Danny.

Mac nodded.

"Want me to check?"

"No," said Mac.

"Wife also has two DUIs," Danny said. "Nothing on the daughter or the boy."

Mac nodded.

Danny knew better than to ask what this information meant, if anything, for their case. Mac would turn the question back on Danny.

Mac got up to go to Sheldon Hawkes' lab. Over his shoulder, he said to Danny, "Let's go get some answers."

Aiden drank green tea. The antioxidants were good for you. Problem was she didn't much like green tea, or any tea for that matter.

Flack was eating a fried egg sandwich with a slice of tomato and Stella had a large orange juice.

"Here it is," Aiden said, handing the file in her hand to Stella. "Want a summary?

"Item," Aiden said. "Asher Glick and Arvin Bloom were in grade school together. May mean nothing.

"Item," she went on, "Arvin Bloom died of brain cancer when he was ten years old. Death records show it."

"Different Arvin Bloom?" asked Flack.

"No," said Aiden. "Childhood address Bloom gave us in Hartford is the same as the one on the death certificate."

"We've got to prove it," said Stella," and even if we do, it doesn't prove he killed anyone. Just stole their identity."

"Look at the photocopy of the birth information," said Aiden.

Stella found it. There were two tiny clear foot-prints.

"So we get prints of the bottom of Bloom's feet and compare them," said Stella.

"Keep going through the folder," said Aiden.

Stella turned over pages as Flack looked over his shoulder. They came to a photograph of a footprint.

"Life size," said Aiden. "Ten and a half. I lifted the print from Bloom's bathroom floor. He was barefoot the last time we searched the shop."

"They don't match," said Stella, "even taking into account the fifty year difference in the ages of these two people." She knew Aiden had examined both prints under a microscope.

"He's going to claim the prints you found in the bathroom aren't his," said Aiden.

"Then we'll ask him nicely for new prints," said Aiden. "And if nicely doesn't work, we get another warrant."

"What else?" asked Stella.

"Had the small splinters of wood on Glick's jacket compared with the sawdust I got from Bloom's shop. Both bloodwood. Tannic acid levels are exact. Magnesium levels are the same. Even the arsenic levels are the same."

"He can talk his way around that," said Flack. "Claim he hugged Glick or something."

Aiden smiled and said, "Then we have the tote bag

Joshua got behind the statue of Jesus in the church. Small specks of wood along the bag's inner lining."

"Bloodwood," said Stella.

"And it matches the other two samples. That bag was in Bloom's shop."

"Motive?" asked Flack.

Aiden nodded toward the folder on the table. Stella flipped through it to five sheets clipped together.

"Summary," said Aiden. "If this guy's our killer it wasn't because of the $40,000 he owed Glick. He has more than eighty thousand in his personal account, about the same amount in his business account and an investment portfolio worth at least $2 million."

"Who the hell is this guy?" said Flack.

"And did he murder two people?" said Stella. "And why?"

Kyle Shelton had been sitting at the window of Scott Shuman's apartment, watching the street. People were moving quickly in spite of the late-morning heat, the New York march.

He drank a can of ginger ale and ate some peanut butter and cheese crackers, deciding when to make his move and where to make it.

The phone on Scott's kitchen counter rang. Kyle didn't pick it up but Scott's answering machine did: "This is Scott Shuman, please leave a message."

When the message clicked off, Scott's voice came on, anxious, concerned: "Kyle, a cop named Taylor just left my office. He asked me if I'd seen you. I told him no. I think he believed me, but you might want to get out of the apartment for a while. Oh, erase this message as soon as you get it, buddy."

As Kyle erased the message, there was a knock at the door. He wondered if whoever was on the other side could hear the machine whirring as it erased. Kyle stood silently.

"Kyle," came a voice he recognized. "We can hear you in there. Open the door, keep your hands in front of you and back up."

It was time. It wasn't the way he had wanted it to come down, but it was one of the ways he had anticipated. He moved to the door, opened it and found himself facing Mac and Danny, both of whom had guns in their hands.

Kyle backed away, his hands showing palms up. Mac and Danny entered and closed the door.

"Your friend Scott is a terrible liar," said Mac.

"He's a good friend," answered Kyle. " 'The most I can do for my friend is to simply be his friend.' "

Kyle paused and said, "Thoreau."

Danny patted Kyle down and told him to sit. As he did, Mac and Danny holstered their weapons.

"He has a vein in his forehead," said Mac. "When he lies it expands."

"Never noticed," said Kyle. "What now?"

"We talk," said Mac.

"You found Jacob?"

"You left me good directions," said Mac.

"Is he okay?" asked Kyle, hand to his cheek.

His face was rough. He hadn't showered or shaved. He had meant to, but had found himself riveted to the chair near the window.

"He'll be fine," said Mac.

"Okay," said Kyle. "I killed them all. Becky, her mother, her father."

"No, you didn't," said Danny.

"What did Jacob tell you?"

"Lies," said Mac. "Lies you taught him."

"Evidence doesn't lie," said Danny.

"You want a lawyer?" asked Mac.

Kyle shook his head "no."

"Let's go over the evidence," said Mac.

The words came silently to Kyle before he could stop or control them. It was happening more often recently, in the last three days, though it had happened for years before.

This time it was the words of La Fontaine: "A person often meets his destiny on the road he took to avoid it."

Sak Pyon was sitting in the CSI lobby when Flack came out of his meeting with Stella and Aiden. Pyon looked anxious, guilty. He held a small brown paper bag and an envelope in his left hand.

Pyon rose as Flack approached him.

"They told me you were in a meeting," Pyon said. "I waited."

Flack nodded.

"You thought of something?" asked Flack.

It was Pyon's day for golf, but he knew from the moment he went to bed the night before that he would not be taking the train to the golf course, not practicing his strokes before placing his tee at the first hole. He would not be losing himself in concentration on the game. He would probably be in jail.

"I did not tell the truth," said Pyon.

Flack didn't answer, so the shorter man continued, "The sketch I gave you did not resemble the man for whom you were looking."

"Why did you do it?"

"He threatened to kill me and my family. He was very convincing. Here."

Flack opened the envelope Pyon handed him and pulled out a pencil sketch that looked nothing like the Hispanic man the shopkeeper had drawn the day before. This sketch looked very much like Arvin Bloom.

"You may have to testify in court," said Flack.

Pyon nodded in understanding and handed Flack the paper bag.

"I was very careful with it," said Pyon.

Danny opened the bag, inside of which was a

plastic bag containing what looked like a paper towel.

Flack looked up.

"That is the paper towel the man you are looking for used in my bathroom after he had threatened to kill my family," said Pyon. "I retrieved it when he was gone."

"Why?" asked Flack.

"You can get DNA from it, can you not? He . . ."

Pyon hesitated, looking for the right word. He mimed blowing his nose.

"He blew his nose on the paper towel?" asked Flack.

"Blew his nose on the paper towel. I heard him. Blew his nose, came out and walked past without looking at me. The man threatened my family," said Pyon. "I wanted to keep something that . . ."

Pyon hesitated.

"Something you could tell him would go to the police if anything happened to you or your family," said Flack.

"Yes," said Pyon with resignation. "Then I realized it would not stop him. I saw it happen in North Korea. He would torture my daughter, my wife in front of me till I gave him the paper towel."

"Thanks," said Flack, bag and sketch in his hand.

"I am free to go?" asked Pyon.

"Have a good day," said Flack.

Flack turned to head back to the room where Stella and Aiden were still meeting.

From behind him, Pyon said, "He spoke Korean to me. Perfect Korean."

Flack looked down at the sketch of Bloom and for the second time in the last hour, Flack asked himself, *Who is this guy?*

The killer had just learned that Joshua had not killed the priest. He had phoned Joshua the day before, told him where to find the tote bag. Joshua had failed, but it might serve the same purpose, assure the police that they had their killer. It was buying him time. The police might come back to him. How much evidence could they get from what they had gathered?

There had been collateral damage. Couldn't be helped. Compared to what he had seen and done around the world, particularly in Asia, this had been a minor setback, but still, he, like all things on earth and in the heavens, was aging.

He would have been gone by now, duffle bag in hand, if there hadn't been a delay at the bank. He had seethed at the ineptitude of the assistant bank manager, but had shown nothing but pleasant patience and understanding.

Though he would have preferred not to, he would now have to make a call to the person who could get him out of this. It had been years since he had called him. It was possible he had been replaced or had retired. Whoever he talked to, he would tell them what had happened. If he didn't they would find out anyway.

Had he forgotten anything? Possibly. He would check again. There wasn't much to get rid of. He had accumulated little and had thrown away what was left in large green plastic bags in Dumpsters blocks away.

If necessary, he would have to lie convincingly. He was well prepared to do so and he was confident he was better at doing it than those who would be coming were at detecting it.

Besides, all he needed was a little more time.

He had two more things that had to be done. Should he first take care of getting rid of what was on the bed above him? Possibly, but he could do that in less than five minutes.

He moved to his computer. He would not just erase everything but remove the hard drive and take it with him. Time to start. He had just typed in the name of his bank, his account number and password when he heard the shop door open.

12

"MAC," COLONEL ANTONIO DENTON SAID, sitting up-right behind his desk in full dress marine uniform. "Give us the evidence and we'll take care of the problem."

The investigation was really Stella and Aiden's, but the connection to Colonel Denton brought Mac into the picture. Besides, he wanted to give both Jacob Vorhees and Kyle Shelton time to think before talking to them again.

The Manhattan office of Colonel Denton was polished walnut from chairs, to floors, to walls, to desk. There were only two photographs on the wall, both signed, one by the first President Bush, the other by a marine private who had signed the full-color photograph of himself and Denton in neat letters: *To Captain Antonio Denton on his birthday, with thanks from a grateful grunt. Semper Fi*. The signature belonged to no one famous, but it was a name both Mac and Denton knew well, a man who had died saving both of the men who now sat in this office.

Denton was fully gray, military cut, average height, a face that had seen much and stored it with loyalty.

"He killed two men," said Mac, handing an envelope over the table to Denton, who was missing the small finger on his right hand.

Denton put on his glasses and looked at the fingerprint record in front of him.

"You got these . . . ?" asked Denton.

"When the suspect had a DUI twenty-two years ago," said Mac. "Name comes up Arvin Bloom, only it's not Arvin Bloom."

They understood each other.

Mac said, "I'd bet these are the only prints on file of the Arvin Bloom who isn't Arvin Bloom. These are the ones that turn up whenever we check his prints."

"And," said Denton, putting down the sheet, "you think the day of this DUI is the day the new Arvin Bloom was born."

"He's off the charts, Tony," said Mac.

Denton nodded. He owed Mac. Mac owed him. It was possible Denton could come up with something. He was military intelligence. It was easier to track such things down since the Homeland Security laws and the "or else" orders for all agencies to cooperate with each other.

"You think he's one of ours," said Denton.

"Kills like it," said Mac. "Possibly military. Possibly CIA."

"Won't be easy," said Denton with a smile.

"Didn't think it would," said Mac. "He's lost it, Tony. He'll kill again."

Denton sat silently for a moment and then said, "As I said, give me what you've got and we'll take care of the problem."

Mac's unblinking look was a familiar one to Denton.

"It's New York's problem," said Mac. "You wouldn't let him walk, but there are others who might depending on what he knows and what he's done. You know it. I know it."

Denton reached for the phone and said, "I'll call you."

Mac nodded and stood up.

"Make it urgent," said Mac. "This one knows how to kill and how to disappear."

"You up for dinner, a drink?" asked Denton.

"Sure," said Mac.

"You holding up all right, Mac?"

They both knew he was referring to 9/11, to Mac's dead wife. Denton had been at the funeral, had stood at Mac Taylor's side.

"Fine," said Mac, forcing a small smile.

"Lieutenant Rivera," said Denton into the phone. "Get me Longretti in Washington."

Mac left the room, closing the heavy door behind him.

Stella had sat at Joshua's bedside, recording his statement, which, she concluded, would probably be worth very little because the man was clearly delirious, guilt-ridden and flashing back to feverish moments in his past.

A physician named Zimmerman, slightly overweight, dressed in whites with the stethoscope of his profession around his neck, watched, fascinated, while his patient was questioned. Zimmerman could not have been more than twenty-eight.

"I killed Glick," said Joshua, wide eyes blinking. "I killed Joel. I was going to kill the priest."

"Go over each murder for me again," said Stella.

Joshua licked his lips and looked at the doctor as if he had never seen the man before.

"I was guided by the hand of a demon," he said.

"Could you be a little more specific than that?" asked Stella.

"Don't remember," said Joshua. "He called me on the phone, found me in a bottle, spoke to me in tongues. Can I request execution by crucifixion in this state?"

"No," said Stella. "Nor in any other one."

"I think he's bleeding again," Dr. Zimmerman said in a deep voice. "Right foot."

Stella nodded, clicked off the tape recorder and tucked it into her kit.

Joshua hadn't killed anyone. A case could be built against Joshua, not a strong one, but one that if taken to a jury might be enough.

Stella rose.

Joshua looked up at her and smiled.

"Anything?" asked Mac, looking through the one-way mirror.

"Lulling 'em. Making nice," said Detective Buddy Roberts, who stood with hands in pockets.

"They say anything?" asked Mac.

"No, Shelton knows we're listening."

Mac's eyes were on Shelton and Jacob Vorhees, who sat silently.

He wasn't looking forward to what was going to happen when he stepped inside that room. He wasn't looking forward to what he was going to do to the frightened boy. Mac told himself that this would hurt Jacob Vorhees, but as with most wounds, after the pain the healing would begin.

Mac looked at Roberts, who shook his head "no" in answer to some inner question.

Roberts, two months from retirement, was big and bald with deep bags under eyes that had seen almost any horror the inhuman mind could come up with. He had built a fragile wall between himself and the images of children mutilated by their own parents, women torn from between their legs up to their bloody faces.

Roberts' wall had been breached a little less than a year ago after he saw the body of a six-year-old boy who had been cut open, his liver removed. The cutter was the boy's father. It was less the horror of the dead boy, which he could block, but the reaction of the father.

"I want to be a liver donor," the father had said with a grin.

The father was a thin weasel with nervous hands and long dirty hair. The reason the father gave for what he had done was that he had been watching a rerun of *Lost in Space* when he suddenly got the idea of cutting out his son's liver. The weasel had thoroughly enjoyed telling the story, and that he had hidden the liver.

Mac had been on the case, had followed a trace trail of blood from the apartment building to a deli across the street. Roberts had watched Mac, who had simply stood inside the deli doorway, looked around and walked to the ice cream freezer. The deli clerk watched as the two policemen removed frozen fruit bars, ice-cream sandwiches, chocolate-topped cones, half gallons and quart blocks of ice cream.

And there it was at the bottom of the case, still

red, frozen inside a zippered see-through bag. Roberts remembered thinking that the liver was no larger than one of the ice-cream sandwiches.

So, when he had interviewed the father, Roberts knew where the liver was: in the CSI lab being examined.

"Freezer at the deli," Roberts had said.

"Good," beamed the father, rubbing his head. "What say we have it for lunch?"

Roberts' wall had not come down completely, but he knew it soon might. He didn't want to see what was on the other side. He had already seen it.

"Buddy?" said Mac, pulling Roberts back from his thoughts.

"Yeah," said Roberts.

"They told them that Shelton can have a lawyer and stop talking and that Jacob must have a lawyer."

Roberts smiled, now fully back in the room.

"Shelton wants no lawyer," said Roberts. "We've got it in writing with witnesses. The Vorhees' family lawyer is on his way here now. We advised the boy that he say nothing till the lawyer gets here."

Mac looked through the window. Shelton looked tired. Jacob looked frightened and determined. Danny said something. Shelton nodded.

A few minutes later there was a knock on the door followed immediately by a lean man of about seventy in a designer business suit. The man who introduced himself as Lawrence Tabler shook Roberts' offered hand.

Mac knew who Tabler was, a high-cost, aggressive and convincing advocate for his clients. He turned his blue eyes on Mac and said, "Detective Taylor."

"Mr. Tabler," Mac acknowledged.

They didn't shake hands. A little over a month after 9/11 Mac had testified as an expert witness in the trial of a man who had brutally beaten his pregnant wife to death.

Tabler had relentlessly attacked the forensic evidence, suggested alternative scenarios to explain the evidence and, finally, attacked the integrity of the entire CSI unit, finishing with Mac. Tabler had done his homework or, more likely, had someone else do it.

"You want my client convicted, don't you, Detective?" Tabler had asked in court.

"He's guilty," said Mac.

"You're sure?" Tabler said, turning to the jury.

"I'm sure."

"Your wife died on 9/11," Tabler said.

"She did."

"You had a breakdown?"

"A short period of clinical depression," said Mac. "Like most people."

"Are you still depressed?" Tabler said, turning back to Mac.

While he didn't look directly at the prosecuting attorney, a slightly plump young blond with long straight hair, Mac did see her, wondered why she hadn't objected to this line of inquiry. Mac knew where it was going and couldn't stop it.

"I'm still depressed," said Mac.

"A man is accused of brutally murdering his wife," said Tabler. "You didn't choose to lose your wife, but you assumed going into the investigation that he had the choice?"

"We work on the evidence," said Mac. "We go where it takes us."

"And this time it took you to my client," said Tabler. "Often evidence doesn't lead. It follows, follows where you want it to take you. Is that right, Detective Taylor?"

"No," Mac had answered firmly.

"You've made mistakes," Tabler pushed.

"Yes," said Mac. He wanted to add, "Haven't you?" but decided not to.

The assistant prosecutor and Tabler made a last-minute plea bargain during the lunch break. Before the judge, the husband had admitted to having taken too many pills for a headache and going wild when his wife had asked him the same question she asked every morning: "One egg or two?"

He had gone into the kitchen and began beating his startled wife.

The plea bargain gave the murderer a minimum

sentence of ten years. Mac felt that the settlement was partly due to his own testimony.

Now Mac said nothing, but opened the door and stepped through with Tabler behind him. Shelton and Jacob looked up.

Tabler smiled at the boy and said, "I'm your lawyer."

Jacob nodded.

"Have you told them anything?" Tabler asked, taking the last chair in the room.

Mac stood against the wall behind Tabler, arms folded.

"He was advised not to say anything till you got here," said Mac.

Tabler tried to turn his head to see Mac, but he couldn't.

Mac went on, "We'd like the two of them to tell us again what happened on the night of the murder."

Jacob pulled a folded sheet of yellow, lined paper from his back pocket and handed it to Tabler, who slowly and carefully read it. When he was finished, he handed the sheet back to Jacob.

"He's already made a statement and signed it," said Mac, moving now to sit next to the lawyer. "And it's on tape."

"Can't be used in court," said Tabler. "He did not have a lawyer present."

"He volunteered," said Mac.

Tabler was shaking his head.

"He's twelve years old. No judge will accept it," Tabler said. "However, I have no objection to reading my client's account of the murder of his family."

Shelton looked past Tabler at Mac, arms folded, sitting across from him. Their eyes met. Kyle Shelton looked away.

Jacob cleared his throat and in a shaking voice read the account he had signed. It was within a few words of being exactly what Jacob had said earlier. Essentially, Jacob recounted hearing noises and a scream. He ran into his sister's room where he saw Kyle Shelton stab his sister and then his mother. Jacob was frozen in horror. Then his father, wearing briefs and a white T-shirt, came into the room and ran toward Shelton, who stabbed him many times. He knew he would get Jacob next. Jacob ran, got his bike and rode away, heading for the woods next to the road. He realized that he was covered with blood. He took off all his clothes and ran naked back to the house through the woods and through backyards. When he got back, Shelton's car was gone. Jacob had gone to the murder scene, saw his family dead and with great difficulty put his mother and sister respectfully on the bed. His father was too big to lift or pull. Then Jacob had heard something—the downstairs door? Had Kyle Shelton come back for him? Jacob ran to his room and groped his familiar way to the closet and climbed up to his private place. He had stayed there for two nights. Then Mac had come with the dog.

"Shelton?" asked Mac.

"What the boy says is the way it happened," he said.

"You have questions, I assume," said Tabler.

"We've got lots of them," said Mac. "I'll start with Jacob."

He moved from the wall, uncrossed his arms and moved toward the table. Jacob raised his right hand as if he were in school.

"Yes?" said Mac.

"How is Rufus? I'd like to see him again," said the boy.

"Who is Rufus?" asked a confused Tabler.

"A dog," said Jacob. "He found my private place."

"I'll see what I can do about you paying Rufus a visit," Mac said.

Mac looked at Jacob and went on.

"I'm going to make some statements and then give you a chance to respond."

"Response will depend on your questions," said Tabler.

Mac nodded and asked his first question.

"Your father had a badly bruised bone in his right forearm. Medical examiner says it happened on the night of the murders. Any idea of how it was broken?"

Jacob shrugged and said, "I don't know."

"Your father was right-handed, right?"

"Yes," said Jacob, looking at Mac as he had been told to do. He had been told not to look at Kyle.

"Would you take off your shoes and socks please?" asked Mac.

"Why?" asked Tabler.

Mac looked at Kyle, who knew exactly why Mac was asking.

"Your client claims to have gone barefoot and naked through the woods for a mile two days ago," said Mac. "I have dated photographs that show the bottoms of his feet with no cuts, bumps or bruises."

"I'd like to see those photographs," said Tabler.

Mac handed the lawyer five eight-by-ten photos of the bottoms of the boy's feet.

"For the record, I'll ask again that your client take off his shoes and socks."

Tabler put down the photos and nodded to the boy to do what he was being asked. When he finished taking off his socks and shoes, Jacob lifted one foot at a time. Tabler and Mac looked. Kyle stared at the wall.

"Your client didn't walk home," said Mac. "He never left his house. Mr. Shelton set up the evidence in the woods to make it look as if Jacob had taken his bike, pedaled down the road, went to the clearing, and left his damaged bike and his clothes there where we could find them."

"How can you conclude that?" asked Tabler.

"From the evidence, particularly a leaf from a linden tree and a crushed caterpillar found in Jacob's room," said Mac, looking at Shelton. "The tree and the caterpillar came from the area where Jacob's bike and clothes were found. We can get leaves from those trees and determine which one the leaf I picked up came from. Since Jacob never left home, the most likely person to have stepped on the leaf is Kyle Shelton. Your turn to take off your shoes, Kyle."

The game was almost over.

"We'll test them for traces of blood from the victims and the dead caterpillar," Mac continued. "If we find traces of the caterpillar, we can match it to the dead one I found on the leaf."

Kyle took off his shoes and handed them to Mac, who placed them on the table.

"Kyle, you want a lawyer now?" asked Mac.

"I suggest you do that," said Tabler.

Kyle shook his head "no."

"Then we go on," said Mac. "We got some of your clothes and did a spectrographic collection of your scent and Jacob's. I got a department dog that specializes in human scent, and let him take his time. Your scent was all over the clearing in the woods. There wasn't the slightest trace of Jacob's scent except on the clothing you left. Then I took the dog to check the Vorhees house. Your scent showed up in the upstairs hallway, on the stairway, in the kitchen, in Becky Vorhees' room and in Jacob's room, but not all over the room, just on a straight line to the closet. You want to tell me why you were in Jacob's room?"

"No," said Kyle, glancing at Jacob and touching the boy's shoulder.

"Okay," said Mac. "I will. Rufus confirmed what I thought. You helped Jacob hide. Why?"

"I was afraid," said Jacob, shaking.

"Jacob," Tabler warned.

"That the police would say I murdered my family," said the boy.

"No," said Mac. "I think Kyle had a plan, not a very good one, too complicated, too many places to find holes full of evidence, too little time to take care of all the holes."

"Detective," Tabler said, looking at Jacob. "My client is through answering questions."

"We checked your father's background," said Mac. "Found out why you've moved so much."

"No more questions," said Tabler.

"I didn't ask a question," said Mac. "I made a statement of fact. The next one is even more important." Mac pulled a photograph of the vase from the box and held it up. Jacob began to cry. Shelton put an arm around him.

"There was a bruise on your father's arm," said Mac. "His right arm. It was sufficient to make him drop whatever he was holding and shatter the vase that he was hit with. Your father was the one with the knife. When you came into your sister's bedroom, she and your mother had already been killed by your father. You grabbed the vase, hit him, took the knife when he dropped it and stabbed him."

Tabler rose and said, "We're leaving."

"No," said Jacob. "We told you what happened."

"The knife wounds on your mother and sister were all approximately the same depth, made by someone considerably stronger than you. The ones on your mother and sister were straight in. The wounds on your father weren't deep and were at an upward angle. They were made by someone much smaller than he was."

"It was me," said Kyle.

"You didn't kill anyone," said Mac.

"I killed many," Kyle said.

"In Iraq," Mac said.

"He's had enough," said Kyle, looking at Jacob, who had taken off his glasses, placed them on the table and leaned against him, his eyes closed and sobbing.

Mac nodded and said to the lawyer, "You should take him in the other room now. A detective will show you where you can have some privacy with your client."

"My client . . ." Tabler began, suddenly sorry that he was involved in this whole mess.

". . . didn't commit any crime except not coming forward as a witness to murder," said Mac. "He killed his father in self-defense. I doubt if a family court judge will do anything but order that he get therapy. I'll recommend it."

"Come with me," Tabler said to Jacob.

The boy continued to cling to Shelton, who handed the boy his glasses and gently urged him out of his chair and toward the lawyer. Jacob put on his glasses and let Tabler guide him out of the room.

"Howard Vorhees came to his daughter's room with a kitchen knife," said Mac. "He came for a sexual attack, threatened her with death. She fought, screamed. He killed her. Jacob heard the noise, ran in just behind his mother. Howard Vorhees killed his wife. That's when Jacob picked up the vase, hit his father's arm, dropped the vase, picked up the knife and stabbed his father."

"How . . . ?"

"Reconstruction from the evidence," said Mac. "That's about when you came through the door, right?"

"Right," he said.

"Wrong," said Mac. "What were you doing there at the exact time of a triple murder in the middle of the night?"

"I was going to be with Becky," he said. "She was expecting me. She left the front door open."

Mac shook his head "no."

"There was a call from Becky's cell phone to yours after two-fifteen."

"She called to ask if I was on the way," he said.

"She was dead, Kyle. Jacob called you and you came to the house and moved the bodies. It took you about half an hour to get there. The trail of blood from the floor to the bed would have shown more blood if Becky and her mother were moved shortly after they were killed."

"Jacob called me," admitted Shelton. "When I got there, he was covered with blood. So was the knife in his hand. He was just standing there looking down at his dead mother. He wasn't concerned with being accused of murdering his family. He was afraid of the world finding out the horror in that house. Better an intruder than the truth. I knew the intruder story wouldn't work. Too much evidence. I sent Jacob to his room and put the bodies on the bed."

"Why?" asked Mac, though he thought he knew the answer.

"It was the right thing to do," Shelton finally said. "Lay out the respected and loved dead and leave a dead dog at their feet."

"Then?" Mac prompted.

"Then I helped Jacob hide, put his bike and clothes in my car, found that wooded area and scattered it all in the clearing."

"You knew we'd find them," said Mac.

"I wanted them found. They were. Without Becky I was going back to a life of grief and despair, a life I had brought home inside me from Iraq. I could live in grief, growing old in low-pay jobs, or I could do it in prison for life and possibly save Jacob. It was worth a try."

"Did you know the leaf was on your shoe?"

Kyle didn't answer.

"You wanted us to find him in the house," said Mac. "But you didn't want to tell us directly and have Jacob think you'd betrayed him. So, you called me, left clues that got more and more simple. The quote you attributed to Anne Frank was obviously not by Anne Frank. You were telling me to look for a child hiding in the house.

"You're guilty of helping to conceal a crime," said Mac. "Considering the crime and why you did it and the fact that you have no record, my guess would be suspended sentence. That's what we'll ask the court for."

"You think they'd let me take care of Jacob?" Kyle asked.

"Stranger things have happened," said Mac, but he didn't believe Kyle getting custody of Jacob would be one of them.

" 'Nobody should pin their hopes on a miracle,' " said Kyle.

"Who said that? Voltaire?" asked Mac.

"Vladimir Putin," answered Kyle.

13

"WE'RE ALMOST BECOMING FAMILY," said Bloom, opening the door to his shop with a look of resignation. "You have a warrant, I assume?"

Stella, Flack and a backup uniformed officer, who looked as if he could be a National Football League lineman, stood in the doorway.

"We're not here to search," said Flack.

Bloom said nothing and waited for them to make their move. Bloom was wearing a pair of neatly pressed navy trousers and a white shirt, also neatly pressed. The clothes did nothing to hide his paunch. He continued to look at them over the rimless lenses of his glasses. Stella thought he looked like anyone's second-favorite uncle.

There was a smell of fresh coffee mingling with the pleasant smell of wood.

"We'd like to talk," said Flack. "Will you please come with us?"

"Can we talk here?" asked Bloom. "I've got coffee brewing."

"We'd like you to come with us," Flack said.

The big uniformed cop shifted his weight, ready to move.

"My attorney has said I should cooperate with you no more," said Bloom. "You'll have to arrest me."

"Sure," said Stella. "You're under arrest for the murders of Asher Glick and Joel Besser."

Bloom shrugged and started forward toward the door.

"Stop," said Stella.

Bloom stopped. Flack's gun was out now. He motioned for the big cop to move forward and pat down Bloom as Flack began to issue the Miranda warning. The cop, whose name was Rossi, was taller than Bloom, easily six foot four. He had been a college wrestler at Rutgers and had tried out for the Steelers, who decided Rossi was just too slow.

"Clean," said Rossi, standing up and taking out his cuffs.

Slump-shouldered Bloom put his hands behind his back. He heard the metal jangle of the handcuffs and made his move. He turned and leveled a sudden sharp chop to Rossi's throat. The big cop went down on his knees, gasping for air, still grasping the handcuffs in his right hand.

Flack stood ready to shoot if the suspect attacked him. The problem was that Bloom had no weapon and Bloom, when he wanted to, could look like a harmless middle-aged man with a paunch and poor eyesight. Shooting unarmed suspects or perpetrators was forbidden except under unusual circumstances. This certainly appeared to be an unusual circumstance.

Flack's hesitation of less than a second would have meant nothing with most people he arrested. Bloom moved with surprising speed, throwing his full weight into Flack, who staggered backward and dropped his gun.

The only one between Bloom and escape was Stella, who stood in the doorway with no expression. She was unarmed.

Bloom had packed a single medium-sized duffle bag, which lay on his bed upstairs. He had taken little time to pack. The delay had been caused by the bureaucracy of the bank. He had called to tell them that he wished to withdraw all of his money, that he would be there within an hour. When he arrived at the bank, the clerk directed him to an assistant bank manager who looked more like a well-dressed young movie star. The assistant manager had assured Bloom that they were almost finished putting together the cash. Over an hour later, Bloom had left the bank with a thickly packed zippered tote bag. The bag was in the trunk of an Altima he had stolen no more than twenty minutes before Stella, Flack and Rossi had appeared at his door. The car was parked in a three-story lot within sight of Bloom's shop.

Now he had to improvise. He had been taught to improvise and over the years had added many improvements on what he had been taught decades ago.

Bloom moved quickly toward Stella. Behind him Rossi's gasps for air sounded like the wheezing of a person in the final throes of emphysema. Flack got to his knees, looked around for his gun and saw it in the left hand of Arvin Bloom.

Kills with his left, writes and eats with his right, thought Stella.

Flack started to stand on shaking legs. Bloom heard the detective over the gasps of the officer on the floor. Bloom turned the gun toward Flack, who started to reach for the backup gun taped to his ankle. Bloom knew just what Flack was doing.

Before the detective could reach his gun, Bloom would shoot him and the woman in the doorway. It would make noise. The shots would probably be called in to 911. He would have to move slowly when he got outside. He couldn't run.

Pain. A terrible pain that sent him into spasms and made him drop to the floor and drop Flack's gun. Bloom, eyes twitching rapidly, looked at Stella and the small black stun gun in her hand. How many volts had she used? He began to writhe on the floor. Flack picked up his gun from the floor where Bloom had dropped it, holstered the gun and cuffed Bloom.

Both Stella and Flack moved to Rossi, whose face was white and bloated. Rossi's mouth was open wide, trying to suck in air. His pleading eyes moved from Flack to Stella.

Flack got on his phone and called for an ambulance, saying, "Officer down."

When he clapped the phone shut, Stella, who was holding Rossi's hand, said, "He needs a tracheotomy, now. Lay him on his back."

Bloom was still writhing, but the spasms had subsided.

Stella had not brought her kit. There had been no thought of crime scene work, only the arrest of a murderer. A mistake. It had been a week of mistakes. Aiden had made a mistake. So had Danny. Now she had made one, too.

The heat, she thought.

"We need a knife or a razor blade," she said. "Something really sharp."

Flack reached into his pocket quickly and glanced at Rossi, whose face was almost a watermelon red. Flack's hand came out with a multi-bladed Swiss Army knife. He opened one of the blades and handed the knife to Stella. She knew how to test the sharpness of a blade without cutting herself. She swiftly ran a finger up the blade toward the edge and past it. Then she looked at the edge of the blade and nodded her head toward Flack.

"We need a straw, a plastic tube, something . . ." she said, but she could see in Flack's eyes that he had seen this before. He could probably even do the tracheotomy, but it was her job.

She looked at Rossi. She was thinking that the young cop's life could now be measured in seconds. Bloom was sitting on the floor, dazed.

"Thin cardboard," she said. "Roll it in a tight tube."

Flack understood. He remembered a tissue box on the counter from the last time he was there. Flack moved behind the counter, found the box and took out the tissues. Then he tore off one side of the box and rolled the cardboard.

"Stella," he called, holding up the tube.

"It'll do," she said.

He gave the rolled-up tube to Stella, who knelt next to Rossi. Rossi's eyes were closing.

"Need me?" Flack asked.

"I'll call if I do," she said.

"Ever done this before?"

"No," she said, lowering the knife toward Rossi's throat.

"Good luck," said Flack, getting up and moving toward Bloom.

A little luck would be great, but Stella believed less in luck than skill. She knew how to do this. She had watched paramedics do it three times. When they were done, she had asked them questions and then later asked Sheldon Hawkes to tell her how it was done.

Stella found the indentation between Rossi's Adam's apple and the cricoid cartilage. Then she made a half-inch horizontal incision about half an inch deep. Rossi didn't react. He didn't seem to be breathing.

Next Stella stuck a finger into the incision. The whole procedure was not only unsterile, but probably profoundly dirty. Couldn't be helped. Blood circled her inserted finger and flowed out of the incision site. Then Stella felt her finger enter the windpipe. With her free hand, she picked up the makeshift cardboard tube and tightened it. It should fit. If not, she would have to make a larger hole if she had enough time.

She carefully removed her finger from the incision and slowly inserted the cardboard tube into the windpipe. She leaned over and blew into the tube to clear it of blood that might have rushed in. Then she waited five seconds and blew into the tube again. She was unaware of where she was and even who she was. She concentrated only on the big police officer. She blew into the tube every five seconds.

"How's it going?" asked Flack.

She didn't answer. She was counting seconds.

Then she heard the warning sound of the paramedic van in the distance. She turned her head toward the street for an instant and then back at the fallen police officer, whose chest was now rising. Less than thirty seconds later, Rossi's eyes opened. He was breathing on his own with pain in his chest and the invasive tube of cardboard in his throat. Rossi mouthed, "Thank you." Stella nodded.

Two paramedics rushed in, kits in hand.

"Where does it hurt?" one of them asked. "Were you shot?"

Stella looked down at her blouse, which was covered with blood, as were both of her hands and her face.

"Not me," she said. "Take care of him. This is his blood."

Both paramedics nodded and moved to Rossi, who, with pain, said, "I can walk."

"Not a good idea," one paramedic said.

"I'm walking," he whispered softly so Flack and Bloom couldn't hear him. "I'm not letting that son of a bitch see me carried out."

They helped him to his feet. He seemed to be breathing normally.

"Nice tracheotomy," said one of the two paramedics. He looked at Stella and added, "You do it?"

Stella nodded.

"You guys are CSI, right? We've seen you before?"

"We're CSI," Stella confirmed.

"All of you?"

"Not the one in cuffs," she said. "He's a murderer."

Rossi gently shook off the hands of the paramedics and managed to walk normally to the door, glancing once at Bloom, who didn't look back at him. The policeman he had hit was unimportant, not worth looking at. It didn't matter that he had lived instead of dying. There had been a few before him, in at least six countries. They were living dots that he could easily erase, witnesses, people who had gotten in the way. They hadn't mattered, since the killing that had been assigned to him had been carried out. Now, for the man who called himself Bloom, the primary thing was staying alive.

He would make a call and they would save him. There was no doubt in his mind. He was too valuable. He knew too much and had hidden documents where even they couldn't find them. They knew that if anything happened to him, he would make a call and someone would bring the documents to *The New York Times*. He would insist that a federal government agency be notified that he had been arrested for murder.

Flack, trying to tame a limp, pushed the big man toward the door. He stopped to pick up Bloom's glasses and was about to put them on the prisoner when he noticed something. He held the glasses up to the light and then handed them to Stella.

She too held them to the light and said, "Plain glass."

Bloom looked over his shoulder at them and smiled.

"Where's your wife?" asked Stella.

Bloom continued to smile.

"Bring him in," she said. "I'll look around here and meet you in about an hour."

She was wrong. It took her two hours in the shop, and that was after she called Aiden, told her what she had found and asked her to bring her kit.

They were in an office in the Manhattan building of family court at Lafayette and Franklin.

Jacob and Tabler sat across from a judge who didn't look much like a judge. She was black, very pretty, with soft-looking ebony hair brushed down to her neck. She couldn't have been more than thirty.

Judge Sandra Whitherspoon had read the reports. Because Jacob was between the ages of seven and twelve, there would be no record of this preliminary hearing or of the case if it went beyond her jurisdiction. In addition, Jacob could not be tried for murder.

She looked up at Tabler and then at Jacob.

"How old were your parents when they were married?" she asked.

The question confused Jacob. Tabler considered saying something but didn't.

"My father was forty-one," he said. "My mother was eighteen."

Judge Whitherspoon nodded as if this were important information.

"Where were they married?" she asked.

"Houston, I think," said Jacob.

"We found your mother's parents in San Antonio," she said. "They want you to live with them. They're coming to get you. I'll be sure they're good people before I release you to them. You understand all this?"

Jacob nodded.

"When you get to San Antonio where they live, they're going to arrange for you to see a psychologist who specializes in children who need help."

Jacob turned to Tabler and said, "What about Kyle?"

"We'll do what we can for him," the old lawyer said gently.

"It's not fair," Jacob said, voice raised, tears in his eyes.

"Why isn't it fair?" asked the judge.

"Because the whole thing was my idea," Jacob said. "He wasn't coming to the house because he was seeing Becky. He came because I called him and asked him to come. When he was on the way I came up with the plan, leaving the evidence in the woods, his running and leaving clues to where I was hiding."

"You talked Mr. Shelton into taking responsibility for a murder he didn't commit?" she said. "And this is the truth?"

Tabler gave up and put his head in his hands.

"The truth," said Jacob.

She didn't believe him. Sandra Whitherspoon and her husband had a twelve-year-old boy and an eight-year-old girl. Sandra Whitherspoon spent her days with children who lied and told the truth and mixed the two, sometimes skillfully. She could detect a child's lie, but she couldn't always prove it.

Truth or lie, she couldn't let the sudden confession pass.

Even if the boy testified in a trial, it wouldn't change the fact that Shelton had broken the law. The information did, however, cause her to rethink the idea of a quick placement of Jacob with his grandparents or anyone else.

She decided to order an immediate psychiatric evaluation.

He sat, hands still cuffed behind him, looking across the table at Aiden and Stella. The look was calm. He could have been a man waiting for the next Amtrak train to anywhere.

Stella nodded at Aiden, who read from a list.

"Bloodwood from your cabinet found on Asher Glick matched. You would have had to touch him."

"We hugged," the man said. "We were old friends."

"The same bloodwood dust was found in the tote bag in the church," Aiden continued.

"There are hundreds of shops in Manhattan that have bloodwood pieces and work in bloodwood flooring and paneling," he said.

This was all a game. He'd play with them until someone appeared to take him out of here. He wouldn't have to call. They would know by now.

"A newsstand owner has drawn a sketch of a man who went through his shop next to the Jewish Light of Christ, threatened the shop owner with death for him and his family if he told about your going through and out the back."

She handed him a copy of the sketch. He looked at it for a few seconds and handed it back without expression. Stella's phone vibrated. She reached into her pocket and flipped it open. It was Mac, who said he was on the way.

"I'd fill you in and let you handle it, but it would take time, and there is some information I can't give you, some information you don't want," he said.

"No problem," she said, looking at the man, whose eyes were on the sketch.

"I'm on the way," Mac said.

Stella and Mac understood each other, coworkers, friends. She flipped the phone closed.

"Looks a little like me," he said. "If, and I only say 'if,' I was in that shop, I didn't threaten the shop owner and I didn't go out of his back door and into the synagogue to kill that man."

"You ever been to Korea?" asked Stella.

He had been expecting this one too. He was well ahead of them.

"No," he said.

"And you don't speak Korean?" asked Stella.

"No," he said.

"The hospital footprints of Arvin Bloom just after he was born don't match yours."

"I don't think a bare footprint match has ever been presented to an American court," he said. "Feet change. Fingerprints don't."

"Don't you want to deny the suggestion that you're not Arvin Bloom?"

"I deny it," he said.

"The fingerprints on Arvin Bloom's identification do match yours," Aiden said. "What did you do for more than forty years?"

"Beachcomber," he said.

Stella and Aiden said nothing.

"In Tahiti," he went on.

"We found her," said Stella.

Bloom understood, but he showed nothing.

"Your wife," said Stella. "Shot in the head twice and stuffed in a zipped-up black body bag under the floor of your bedroom. You're a good wood-worker."

"I'd like to make a phone call now," he said calmly.

Stella put her cell phone on the table in front of him, got up and took off the handcuffs. He rubbed his wrists and reached for the phone. Yes, they would later check the phone log and find the number he had called, but it would make no difference. He could have insisted on using a public phone, but that too would be traced. He could have insisted on privacy, but he didn't need it.

Stella remained behind him as he punched in the number. The phone rang and a recorded voice message said, "I'm sorry but the number you have dialed is no longer in service. If you think you have dialed incorrectly, please hang up and try again."

He closed the phone and placed it on the table.

This was wrong. Why had they cut him off? They knew he could make another call and copies of the documents would resound on the front page of the *Times*, lead off the evening news, cost a lot of people their government jobs.

"Hands," said Stella behind him.

This wasn't a perfect time, but he might not get another. And what did he have to lose? Neither woman was armed. Outside the door, to the left, down a short corridor, was an emergency exit door.

He struck out at the woman behind him, the woman who had shot him with a Taser. At the same time he pushed the table over on the other one.

He made the short dash to the door. Once on the street, he would know how to hide. He might have to do more killing, but he knew how to hide and how to survive.

He opened the door and Mac Taylor punched him hard. The blow broke his nose. The man who had been calling himself Arvin Bloom stepped back, didn't raise a hand to his nose. He charged Mac, who faked a punch to the head.

The man instinctively reached up to protect his broken nose. Mac's punch was to the man's solar plexus. The man went down hard, dazed, to a sitting position on the floor.

"You both okay?" Mac asked.

Stella was standing a few feet away, her Taser in hand.

"Sore shoulder," she said.

Aiden was picking up the table.

"I'm fine," she said.

Stella snapped the cuffs on behind the back of the man, whose nose was now gushing blood. He stood up.

"He doesn't give up," she said, leading the man back to the chair behind the table.

Aiden turned, reached into her kit and came up

with large gauze pads. When the man was seated, she pressed the pads against his bloody nose.

"He can't afford to. His name is Peter Moser," said Mac, who leaned over, his face inches away from the man, and said, "I have another name you might be interested in: Harry Eberhardt."

They knew who he was and he knew who had told them. They had found Eberhardt, which meant that his ace in the hole, the documents, had been found and probably destroyed. No more leverage.

"How did you find him?" Moser said.

"You said that you'd sold the bloodwood cabinet yesterday," said Mac. "You didn't know who you sold it to. It was a heavy piece."

"It took at least two people to move it," said Aiden.

Moser looked up. He would find a way to get out of this. He had been in worse situations.

"We checked for fingerprints on the pieces near where the bloodwood cabinet had been. Lots of prints. One set in particular, fingers and palm, as if someone had put his hand against the wall to get some leverage to move the cabinet away from the wall. The print wasn't good enough to run through the system. The fingers and palm that made it were worn by acid and chemicals."

Moser was breathing heavily through his mouth.

"The print had traces of chemicals we don't usually find on fingerprints," Mac went on. "Monomethyl-p-aminophenol sulfate, acid, sodium hydroxide, potassium bromide. Know who uses those chemicals?"

Moser knew but said nothing.

"Photographers," Mac said. "They use it for developing and printing. Photographs are almost all digital now. Drugstores, photo supply stores do develop film, but the processing is all done by computerized machines. The only ones who still process their own film are professional photographers, the ones who do portraits, landscapes, homes, some weddings, fashion, upscale catalogues."

Moser didn't answer. Aiden, now wearing latex gloves, took the blood-soaked pad from Moser's nose, dropping it into a bag. The bleeding had slowed. She pressed a fresh pad on his nose. When it began to slip, she taped it to his face.

"We could have checked them all out," Mac went on, "but we didn't have to. We looked for those close enough to your shop so two men could carry that cabinet."

"Block and a half down from his shop," said Stella, remembering.

"Harry Eberhardt, photographer," said Mac. "We found the bloodwood cabinet in the room behind Eberhardt's studio. There's also a darkroom. Detective Flack told him you were facing three charges of murder and that one of the victims was the woman you had shot a few hours ago. Eberhardt gave me the sealed envelope. A representative of the federal government has it now."

Moser looked straight ahead.

Mac turned to Stella to take over.

"We were wrong," she said. "You didn't kill Asher Glick because you owed him money. You killed him because he had come into your shop. You gave him your name, told him you were Bloom, told him where you were supposedly from. He probably asked more questions about your youth. You would have done your homework, given all the right answers, but Glick knew you weren't Bloom. Your bad luck was running into someone who knew the real Arvin Bloom when he was a boy, knew you weren't him, knew he was dead."

"You probably made up a story," said Mac. "A good one, but not good enough. He had told you about the morning *minyan*. You promised to be there and bring evidence that you were telling the truth about your story."

"You got him alone," said Stella. "Improvised, killed him and tried to make it look like a ritual killing. And then when we came to you as a suspect you were afraid we'd dig and find out you were a fraud. So you decided to kill again, another Jew, in the same ritual way, a victim with whom you had no connection. The Hebrew words in chalk had no meaning. You probably got them off the Internet. Then you found . . ."

". . . a good person to take the fall," said Mac. "Joshua."

None of the three investigators said a word for a full minute. Stella sat unblinking, looking at Moser. Aiden's arms were crossed as she eyed Moser with disgust. Mac laid his palms flat on the table.

There was a knock at the door and Jane Parsons entered. She was wearing her white lab coat and carrying a single sheet of paper, which she handed to Mac, who read it and then handed it to Stella, who, in turn, handed it to Aiden. Jane looked at the bleeding man, but seemed to have no reaction.

Moser showed no interest in what was going on. If he went to trial he would be convicted. The evidence was overwhelming. He would go to prison. That was a certainty. He might even get the death penalty. If he made a deal and confessed to avoid the death penalty, he doubted if they would let him survive more than a few weeks or months in prison, but he had a good deal to make. Even without the evidence Eberhardt had turned over to the police, Moser knew enough—names, dates, events—to cause havoc. They couldn't let that happen, couldn't let him go public. He would either have to escape within the next few days or be killed.

Mac looked at Jane. She looked tired. They were all tired and hot and sweaty.

"Thanks," he said.

Jane smiled. She had been doing that more often recently. Then she left the room.

"Good news," Stella said, looking at Moser, who couldn't keep from looking up.

They've decided to come through for me, Moser thought. He would be back on the street before the day was over and then he would have to hide before someone put two bullets in his head.

"We're removing the charge of murdering your wife from the list of charges," Stella said.

Moser's mouth tightened slightly under the bloody pad.

"Want to know why?" asked Mac.

Silence.

"Because," said Aiden, "the woman you killed in your bedroom wasn't your wife. She was your sister."

Moser probably wouldn't even be safe in an isolated, guarded, secured location, the kind where they put mob hit men who talk to save their lives, have someone ghostwrite their largely invented memoirs, watch television and stay alive. It was worth a try.

"I want to make a deal," Moser said.

"We don't have the authority to make deals," said Mac.

"Find me someone who does," said Moser.

"What do you have to deal with?" asked Aiden.

Moser looked at them individually with a tilt of his head and a ghastly smile and said, "Thirty-seven assassinations for a government agency, assassinations in nine countries, most of them in Korea, North and South."

"One question," said Aiden. "Why cabinetmaking?"

"It's a perfect meditation," said Moser. "Creating objects of utility and beauty with your hands touches the soul and confirms the wonder of the universe."

"We ran your sister's fingerprints and came up with a match for a Lily Drew from Cleveland," said Stella. "The Cleveland police found your aunt and uncle. We're going to have them identify you. You used your sister as a front and when you decided to run, you killed her. Anything you want to say, Evan Drew?"

Mac and Danny had peeled away the identities of the man, enough to find the core.

Evan Drew, a.k.a. Peter Moser, a.k.a. Arvin Bloom sat silently staring at the pale wall, where he made out a face in the plaster, the face of an almost skeletal man, mouth open, crying out. He had seen such things all over the world, mostly in bathroom floors. He did not ask but he was sure others did not see the haunting images.

"I need a doctor," said Drew.

The interrogation was over. Less than an hour later word came that the district attorney's office was not interested in making a deal with Evan Drew.

Sitting in a holding cell, Drew began to rethink his options. There were few. There may not have been any.

14

In the more than fifty years he had lived in the neighborhood, it was the first time Rabbi Benzion Mesmur had been in St. Martine's Church, which was no more than a five or ten minute walk from his synagogue and less than that from his home. Father Wosak had invited him for coffee and cookies, which, the priest assured him, had both been purchased at Kauffman's Kosher Bakery.

"If you'd prefer that I come to you . . ." the young priest had begun when they spoke on the phone.

The rabbi knew from the tone that he was deferring to the older man's age and his position in the community.

Wosak had made the request in Hebrew. He had also given Rabbi Mesmur a choice of times that would not interfere with his duties.

The old rabbi, in a black suit on the hottest day of the year, had walked to the church with two members of his congregation, both of whom were over seventy, both of whom had asked him to allow himself to be driven. The rabbi had said, "No, thank you."

The two men who had accompanied the rabbi remained outside when their rabbi entered St. Martine's.

After they had finished their coffee and cookies, the priest said, in English, "I have a request."

The old man waited.

"I'd like our congregation to pray for Asher Glick at this Sunday's service," Father Wosak said.

"You don't need my permission," said Rabbi Mesmur.

"I do," said the priest.

"Then you have it," said the rabbi.

"My sermon on Saturday will be on Jesus the Jew," said Wosak.

Both men thought about Joshua in the hospital, Joshua who outwardly said he could bridge the massive canyon of belief between the two religions, but inwardly knew he was a false prophet.

"And the other one?" asked the rabbi.

"We'll pray for Joel Besser too," said Wosak.

Rabbi Mesmur stroked his beard once and nodded.

For the next twenty minutes the two men discussed the meaning of God's destruction of the sons of Aaron, who had come too close to the altar. Their interpretations were remarkably close.

A sound beyond the priest's sanctuary door made him rise and say, "Excuse me."

Rabbi Mesmur also rose and followed the priest to the door.

Stella had volunteered to tell the two men about catching the murderer and about the motive for the crime.

When the two clergymen stood in the open door looking into the church, they saw Stella alone, kneeling before the altar, hands clasped, head down in prayer.

Father Wosak closed the door and the two men left Stella to her prayer.

At five p.m. Danny Messer handed the paperback book through the bars to Kyle Shelton. Kyle had asked if it were possible for the book to be brought to him from his apartment.

"Thanks," said Kyle.

He was freshly shaved, hair combed back, orange prisoner uniform unwrinkled. Kyle stood straight. Stoic. Military. Kyle Shelton, former PFC, who had served in an infantry unit in Iraq, had found a comfort zone, Danny thought. Danny's comfort zone was his work. Danny found it ironic. The very thing he loved the most had taken him to the edge of a breakdown.

There was someone sleeping, or trying to sleep, in one of the two bunks behind Shelton. The man in the bunk was covering his eyes with his left arm to keep out the sun.

The air-conditioning had been turned down to save money, or perhaps the system was overworked. It must have been about ninety degrees in the cell. The dampness and heat had brought out the worst of the smells of the cells—long-dead cigarettes that lingered, human sweat that was a cacophony of alcohol and lingered for days, essence of vomit, and the hint of something or someone who had died.

The heat had laid out the man on the bunk, but Shelton was not sweating; not a spot of perspiration darkened his prison uniform.

"Ever read this?" asked Kyle.

He held up the book, *The Conquest of Happiness* by Bertrand Russell.

"No," said Danny.

Kyle opened the book, found what he was looking for and read: "Life is not to be conceived on the analogy of a melodrama in which the hero and heroine go through incredible misfortunes for which they are compensated by a happy ending. I live and have my day, my son succeeds me and has his day, his son in turn succeeds him. What is there in all this to make a tragedy about?"

Kyle closed the book, held it up and said, "Thank you."

Danny nodded.

"You like to take a look at this when I'm finished with it?" Kyle said.

Danny said, "Yes."

At five p.m. Detective Donald Flack, hands at his sides, stood in front of the isolated cell in which Drew sat on the lone cot, looking at the wall. He did not acknowledge the presence of the detective.

Flack's ribs stung with sudden pain unless he walked slowly and didn't move his arms too much. Even a deep breath caused him to wince. The pain was worse than it had been during most of the time since Drew had run into him. The ribs were bruised, but some of them were the same ones that had been broken by another killer on a day as cold as this one was hot.

Neither man spoke. There was nothing more to say. Flack had come only to show that he had not been hurt by Drew's rush at him in the shop. The detective, stone-faced, looked at the man who had come very close to killing him—and there was little doubt that Drew would have killed him if he had taken a shot. The man was an assassin who, if he were to be believed, had murdered thirty-seven people. Flack believed the big, paunchy man with a monk's large bald patch and graying hair. Flack remembered how quickly the man had moved in his shop to take down both Rossi and Flack.

Drew didn't seem to notice Flack. He might have been faking it, but from the look on the prisoner's face, Flack thought that the man was crawling into himself. Flack had seen it before, but he knew it wasn't always safe inside that shell. One multi-murderer had told him about going into the shell but being driven back out by the sound of an ocean of agonized voices.

Drew smiled almost to himself and reminded Flack of someone else: Norman Bates.

After five minutes, Flack walked away slowly, hiding the pain in his chest.

Drew was thinking in Korean, trying to remember the name of the labor leader he had killed in Thailand. He did not know why he felt the need to remember, but he knew it was not because of guilt. If he were to find peace for even a short time, he would have to remember. If he were to remember, he would be able to meditate, but he couldn't. This had never happened to Evan Drew before. He couldn't control it. If only he remembered the man's name, he could go back to his meditation. He could see the man inside the restaurant. The man had been laughing, chopsticks in hand, when Evan Drew had shot him through the window.

The name suddenly came to him, but the relief

he hoped for didn't come. He now had to know the exact number the man had been on the list of his killings.

At five p.m. Stella Bonasera sat in her living room, a glass of iced tea in her hand, the air conditioner turned up.

She looked at one of the paintings on the wall. George Melvoy had admired her paintings. He had intruded, changed the meaning of her space forever. She felt no anger. Melvoy was getting better, but he was going to suffer, at least until the Alzheimer's erased the memories of loss and pain.

She didn't want him to suffer. He was a proud old man who had suffered enough in his life. He didn't need Stella's anger. He didn't need Stella's forgiveness. She looked at the painting that she knew Melvoy had moved slightly when he brought the poison.

Stella had bought the painting in Antwerp two years ago. The painting was bright, a black road with thick fields of yellow flowers growing on both sides, the sun just setting in the distance; a glowing object was moving toward the sun, which would never set. You couldn't tell by looking at the painting, but the glowing object was a human being.

No deduction here. The painter, Mary-Celeste Kouk, had told her. Mary-Celeste was emaciated and wide-eyed and wearing a pair of very worn jeans and a red shirt with long sleeves and a John Deere logo. Stella was certain the shirt covered the clear evidence of the painter's drug habit. Mary-Celeste set up her paintings on the banks of a canal next to a bridge.

"The painting comes with a secret," the woman had said. "That glowing orange dot was me. Now it is you."

Stella was on a long flight toward the sunset. She found comfort in this and the iced tea.

At five p.m. Aiden and her friend Karen Dukes, who worked in the ballistics lab, were having dinner at a Japanese restaurant on Second Street.

This was a rarity in both of their lives, a night out in which they could have ethnic food and go to a movie, a comedy. Neither woman could watch horror or superhero or street gang movies. They could eat slowly, talk about anything but work. Then they would see the movie. Aiden could not remember which Wilson brother was in it or who the other star was. It didn't matter as long as it was funny or even tried to be.

Aiden's motto for at least the next few hours was "Forget the day."

"What's that?" asked Karen when Aiden reached over to pick up her soup spoon.

Aiden looked at her hand. The first finger on her right hand was red and swollen.

"Splinter," said Aiden.

"It's in there?" asked Karen.

"It is," said Aiden, starting her soup.

"You should have it taken out," said Karen.

"I took antibiotics," said Aiden. "It should take care of a possible infection. If not, I'll take it out."

"You want it to stay inside you?" asked Karen.

"Yes," said Aiden.

"In the name of heaven, why?"

"To remind me of something," said Aiden. "The soup is good."

"Very," said Karen. "What's in your finger?"

"A very small splinter of bloodwood."

At five p.m. Jacob Vorhees was asleep in Juvenile Detention. He did not dream. He dared not dream. He had gone to sleep thinking not of his family, but of Rufus. Later, in the relative safety of a therapist's or social worker's office, he might be able to talk about what had been done, what he had done. For now, however, he could think only of the dog.

At five p.m. Danny Messer was home showering. He had been given two weeks' mandatory leave with pay and with the possibility of an extension.

He had to see Sheila Hellyer for half an hour every day for those two weeks. That was fine with him.

The tremor was gone. Hot water beat soothingly

on his head and down his back. He heard himself humming, surprised that he was looking forward to the next two weeks.

He had promised himself that someday he would read *War and Peace*. Now would be a very good time, but then again, the Mets were opening a home series with the Cardinals tomorrow night.

At five p.m. Joshua lay in his hospital bed trying without success to understand what had happened to him. They had given him shots of morphine for his pain. Suddenly he experienced an epiphany. His way was not religion. He had served it badly and it had served him badly. It was not his calling. He needed a cause, a real-world cause, a new group of the devoted young around him. If Communism were the least bit viable, Joshua would have become a Communist at that very second.

Animal rights. That was it. He smiled and imagined all the abuse taken by cows, ducks, horses, chickens, turkeys, seals, whales, pigs, even fish. I'm a vegetarian, he thought. From this moment, I'm a vegetarian. He closed his eyes.

At five p.m. Jane Parsons and Mac Taylor were sharing a pizza at a hole in the wall with three tables. Most of the trade was pizza by the slice to go.

They had both agreed on double cheese, onions and anchovies.

There was a ceiling fan spinning and wobbling dangerously, providing almost no relief from the heat of the ovens, which added to that of the air coming in through the open door.

The plan was to finish the pizza and the Diet Cokes and get back to work. Jane had DNA orders piled up at least two inches high. Mac had the gun Evan Drew had used. He planned to send e-mails to Interpol which, in turn, would send the request to its 184 members around the world, asking if they had any unsolved murders from before eight years ago involving two shots in close proximity to the back of the head with bullets from a small-caliber gun.

Someone behind the counter was shouting to someone behind him to make a large sausage-and-onion to go. Jane and Mac were silent as they ate. Then, pizza finished, she put her hands together and touched them to her lips, saying, "Tell me about your wife."

Talking about Claire was not easy. Usually he simply didn't do it, but in this loud, hot pizza shop he began talking. He was surprised that it didn't hurt. He was surprised by Jane's attentiveness. He told her things that he had not told anyone, including himself, since 9/11.

Outside it began to rain and, for a few minutes at least, it was cool in New York.